A Christmas Odyssey

A Christmas Odyssey

A Novel

Anne Perry

BALLANTINE BOOKS · NEW YORK

Copyright © 2010 by Anne Perry

Published in the United States by Ballantine Books, an imprint of The Random House Publishing Group, a division of Random House, Inc., New York.

BALLANTINE and colophon are registered trademarks of Random House, Inc.

LIBRARY OF CONGRESS CATALOGING-IN-PUBLICATION DATA
Perry, Anne.
A Christmas odyssey : a novel / Anne Perry.
p. cm.
ISBN 978-0-345-51858-3 (hardcover : alk. paper)
ISBN 978-0-345-52317-4 (ebook)
1. Fathers and sons—Fiction. 2. Police—England—London—Fiction.
3. Missing—Fiction. 4. Christmas stories. 5. London (England)—Social conditions—19th century—Fiction. I. Title.
PR6066.E693C4725 2010
823'.914—dc22   2010033239

Printed in the United States of America on acid-free paper

www.ballantinebooks.com

2 4 6 8 9 7 5 3 1

FIRST EDITION

Text design by Julie Schroeder

*D*edicated to all who look upward

A Christmas Odyssey

*H*ENRY RATHBONE LEANED A LITTLE FARTHER forward in his armchair and regarded his visitor gravely. James Wentworth had an air of weariness in his face that made him look older than his sixty-odd years. There was something close to desperation in the way his hands fidgeted, clenching and unclenching on his knees.

"What can I do?" Henry asked gently.

"Perhaps nothing," Wentworth answered. As he spoke, the logs in the fire settled deeper, sending up a shower of sparks. It was a bitter night, ten days before Christmas. Outside, the icy wind moaned in the eaves of this pleasant house on Primrose Hill. Beyond, the vast city of London prepared for holiday and feasting, carols, church bells, and parties. There was not long to wait now.

"You say 'perhaps,'" Henry prompted him. "So possibly there is something to be done. Let us at least try." He gave a brief smile. "This is the season of hope—some believe, of miracles."

"Do you?" Wentworth asked. "Would you pursue a miracle for me?"

Henry looked at the weight of grief in his friend's face. They had not met in more than a year, and it seemed that Wentworth had aged almost beyond recognition in that time.

"Of course I would," Henry replied. "I could not promise to catch it. I cannot even swear to you that I believe in such things."

"Always honest, and so literal," Wentworth said with a ghost of amusement in his eyes.

"Comes from being a mathematician," Henry answered. "I can't help it. But I do believe there is more to be discovered or understood than the multitude of things that we now know all put together. We have barely tasted the realm of knowledge that lies waiting."

Wentworth nodded. "I think that will suffice," he accepted. "Do you remember my son, Lucien?"

"Of course." Henry remembered him vividly: a handsome young man, unusually charming. Far more than that, he was filled with an energy of mind and spirit, an insatiable hunger for life that made other people think of new horizons, even resurrect old dreams.

Pain filled Wentworth's eyes again and he

looked down, as if to keep some privacy, so as not to be so acutely readable.

"About a year ago he began to frequent certain places in the West End where the entertainment was even more . . . wild, self-indulgent than usual. There he met a young woman with whom he became obsessed. He gambled, he drank to excess, he tasted of many vices he had not even considered previously. There was an edge of violence and cruelty in his pursuits that was more than the normal indulgence of the stupidity of a young man, or the carelessness of those with no thought for consequences."

He stopped, but Henry had not interrupted him. The fire was burning low. He took two more logs from the basket and placed them on the embers, poking them to stir up the flames again.

"Now he has disappeared. I have tried to look for him myself," Wentworth continued. "But he evades me, going deeper into that world and the darkness of those who inhabit it. I . . . I was angry in the beginning. It was such a waste of the talent and the promise he had. To begin with, when it was just overindulgence in drinking and gambling, I forgave him. I paid his debts and even saved him from prosecution. But then it grew far worse. He became violent. Had I gone on rescuing him, might I have given him to believe that there is no price to be paid for cruelty, or that self-destruction can be undone at a word, or a wish?" His hands gripped each other, white-knuckled. "Where does forgiveness eventually become a lie, no longer an issue of his healing but simply my refusal to face the truth?"

"I don't know," Henry said honestly. "Perhaps we seldom do know, until we have passed the point. What would you like me to do?"

"Look for Lucien. If I go after him myself, I only drive him deeper into that terrible world. I am afraid that he will go beyond the place from where he could ever return, perhaps even to his death." He looked up, meeting Henry's eyes. "I realize how much it is I ask of you, and that your chances of success may be slight. But he is my son. Nothing he does changes that. I deplore it, but I shall not cease loving him. Sometimes I wish I could; it would be so much easier."

Henry shook his head. "Those of us who have loved don't need an explanation, and those of us who haven't would not understand it." His smile was rueful, with a little self-mocking in it. "I study science and logic, the beauty of mathematics. But without those things that are beyond explanation, such as courage, hope, and above all, love, there can be no joy. I'm not even sure if there could be humor. And without laughter we lose proportion, perhaps in the end even humanity."

He became serious again. "But if I am to look for Lucien, I need to know more about him than the charming young man I met, who was apparently very well able to hide the deeper part of himself from superficial acquaintances, perhaps even from those who knew him well."

Wentworth sighed. "Of course you must. That is still not to say that I find it easy to tell you." He sighed. "Like most young men, he explored his physical appetites, and to begin with I did not find his excesses worrying. I can remember being somewhat foolish myself, in my twenties. But Lucien is thirty-four, and he has not outgrown it. Rather, he has indulged more dangerous tastes: drugs of different sorts that release all inhibitions and to which it is all too easy to become addicted. He enjoys the usual pleasures of the flesh, but with young women of a more corrupt nature than most. There is always the danger of disease, but the woman he has chosen is capable of damage of a far deeper sort."

For a few moments Wentworth stared into the flames, which were now licking up and beginning to devour the new logs. "She offers him the things he seems to crave most: a feeling of power, which is perhaps the ultimate drug, and of being admired, of being able to exercise control over others, of being regarded as innately superior."

Henry did not argue. He began to see the enormity of what his friend was asking of him. Even if he found Lucien Wentworth, what was there he could say that might tempt him to come back to the father he had denied in every possible way?

"I'll try," he said quietly. "But I have little idea how to even begin, let alone how to accomplish such a task."

"Thank you," Wentworth replied, his voice hoarse. Perhaps he was finally facing the reality that to try at all was little more than a kindness, driven by pity rather than hope. He rose to his feet as if exhaustion all but overwhelmed him. "Thank you, Henry. Call if you have anything to tell me. I shall not disturb you to ask." He put one hand in a pocket and pulled out a piece of paper. "Here is a list of the last places that I know he frequented. It may be of use."

*H*enry Rathbone awoke the following morning wishing that he had not promised Wentworth that he would help him. As he sat at the breakfast table, eating toast and marmalade without pleasure, he admitted to himself that it was a lack of courage that had made him agree to it. Even if Henry found him, Lucien Wentworth was not going to come home. He did not want to. His father might be spared a good deal of distress simply by not knowing for certain what had happened to him.

But Henry had given his word, and now he was bound to do his best, whatever that might turn out to be. How should he begin? He had had a good deal of fun in his own university days, which were now at least thirty-five years behind him. He had sat up all night talking, certainly drunk more beer than was good for him, knew some women of a sort his mother didn't even imagine existed, and learned some very bawdy songs, most of which he still remembered.

But he had grown out of it before he was thirty. It was all a hazy memory now, which was not even worth exploring. What compelled Lucien was something entirely different. It was a hunger that fed upon itself and that, in the end, would devour everything.

He spread out the sheet of paper Wentworth had given him, the list of places he had found Lucien in the past. But by his own admission Lucien was no longer likely to be in such places. He had sunk deeper than mere drunken brawling and abuse, or even the simple womanizing many young men indulged in at the better-known brothels.

Many of his own friends had sons who had disappointed them, one way or another, but a good man did not ask questions about such things, and if he accidentally learned of them he affected not to have. He certainly did not repeat it to others.

❧

*H*enry's own son, who was perhaps London's most brilliant barrister, had been both admired and deplored, depending upon whom he had represented most recently. He had also, at times, behaved in ways that Henry found difficult to understand, and would certainly not have wished to discuss with anyone outside the family—except perhaps Hester Monk. It had never been a matter of overindulgence. Actually he wondered at times if it might not have been better for Oliver to have let himself go occasionally, even at the cost of an error or two!

Once, Henry had hoped Oliver would marry Hester, but he had realized some time ago that it would not have made Hester happy. She needed a man of more will and passion, like William Monk. Whether or not Hester would have made Oliver happy he was less certain. He thought perhaps she might have, but of course it was far too late now.

However, Hester might be able to advise Henry in his quest for Lucien, and he could be honest with her. There would be no need for any pretense, which would be exhausting, and in the end also self-defeating.

Hester had been a nurse in the Crimea during that wretched war, which was now—at the end of 1865—a decade gone into history. On her return home, she had initially dreamed of reforming nursing in England, in line with Florence Nightingale's beliefs. However, the world of medicine was powerful, and unready for such advances. Hester had been obliged to seek one position after another in private nursing. Then she had married Monk, and found it difficult to work so far from

11

home. As his work prospered, she had opened the clinic in Portpool Lane where she and others nursed women of the street who could find no other medical care for their most desperate needs. The funds came from charitable donations. Through these experiences, Hester might well have access to the kind of knowledge that Henry now needed.

With a little spring in his step he increased his pace along the wet, windy street and hailed a hansom cab.

"Portpool Lane, if you please," he requested, climbing up and seating himself comfortably. It was not a long ride, even though the traffic was growing denser as the light faded in the winter afternoon.

"Right y'are, Guv," the driver said briskly, urging his horse forward along the Strand, and then left up Chancery Lane.

The street lamps were being lit already. It was not long until the shortest day of the year, and they traveled in the murk of smoke and drifting rain. Henry could hear the clatter of hooves, the jingle of harness, and the hiss of wheels on the wet cobbles.

"Happy Christmas!" a man called out cheerfully, his voice rising above the cries of peddlers and curses of those caught up in tangles of traffic.

"You too!" came back the reply.

"Get on, yer fool!" someone else yelled out, caught behind a slow-moving dray, and there was a roar of laughter.

"Happy Christmas to you too!"

They turned right briefly up High Holborn, and then left on Gray's Inn Road. Just past the square Henry rapped with his cane to catch the driver's attention. "This will be excellent, thank you. I can walk the rest of the way."

"Right, sir," the driver said with some surprise. "'Appy Christmas, sir."

Henry paid him, adding a rather generous tip, prompted by the well wishes, even though he knew they were given for precisely that purpose.

He crossed the road to the entrance of Portpool Lane and stepped onto the narrow path with confidence. The street lamps were few, and the vast dark mass of Reid's Brewery dominated the farther end, but he knew his way.

❧

*I*nside the clinic, Squeaky Robinson was sitting at the table going over the accounts. It was his profession to keep the books—not that it had always been so. In the previous incarnation of the building he had owned it, and run it as a very successful brothel. He had been tricked out of its ownership by William Monk and Oliver Rathbone, Sir Oliver, as he now was.

The loss of it meant that Squeaky, in his later middle years, had become homeless and penniless in the same instant. What was worse, he even stood in some danger of going to prison. That was a fate he had managed to avoid all his life, from childhood pocket-picking, with great skill—none of your ordinary stuff—right through his whole career until he owned this warren of buildings and made a handsome profit from them.

But those days were over, and he greatly preferred not to think of them. He was now a perfectly respectable man, keeping the books and managing the offices of the Portpool Lane Clinic for Hester Monk, who was a lady of spirit, considerable intelligence, and formidable will.

His attention was on the next column of figures when the door opened and a tall, lean gentleman came in, closing it behind him to keep out the bitter weather. Squeaky used the word "gentleman" in his mind, because years of experience had taught him to estimate a man's social standing at a glance, and also to make a pretty accurate guess as to his intentions. In the past, his life had occasionally depended on that, and old habits died hard. This man he judged to be a gentleman by nature, possibly middle-class by birth, and a scholar by occupation. This estimate he drew from his unpretentious but well-cut clothes, his mixture of modesty and confidence, and the very slight stoop of his shoulders.

"Mornin' sir," he said curiously. "Can I help you?"

"Good morning," the man replied pleasantly. His voice reminded Squeaky of someone, but he could not recall who. "My name is Henry Rathbone. I would very much like to speak with Mrs. Monk. If she is here, would you be good enough to ask her if that is possible?"

Of course: He must be Sir Oliver's father. That was the resemblance. Now why would he be here to see Miss Hester? Squeaky regarded him more closely. He had a mild, agreeable face, but there was nothing passive about those blue eyes. A very clever man, Squeaky judged, possibly very clever indeed, but—at the moment—also a worried man. Before he let him in to see Hester, Squeaky would like very much to know what he wanted so urgently that he came all the way from wherever he lived to a place like Portpool Lane.

"She's helpin' patients right now," he replied. "We had a bad night. Big catfight down Drury Lane, knives an' all." He saw the gentleman's look of pity with satisfaction. "Mebbe I can help? In the meantime, like."

Rathbone hesitated, then seemed to come to some decision. "It is advice I need, and I believe Mrs. Monk may be able to guide me toward someone who can give it to me. When might she be free?"

"Is it urgent?" Squeaky persisted.

"Yes, I'm afraid it is."

Squeaky studied the man even more closely. His clothes were of excellent quality, but not new. This suggested that he cared more for substance than appearance. He was sure enough of himself not to have any hunger to impress. Squeaky looked into the clear blue eyes and felt a twinge of unease. He might be as gentle as he seemed, but he would not be easy to fool, nor would he be put off by lies. He would not have come to Hester for medical help; he would most certainly have his own physician. Therefore it was help of some other sort that he wanted: perhaps connected with the clinic, and the kind of people who came there.

"Mebbe I can take a message to her?" Squeaky suggested. "While she's stitching and bandaging, like. Is it about the kind o' folk what come here?" It was a guess, but he knew immediately that he had struck the mark.

"Yes, it is," Henry Rathbone admitted. "The son of a friend of mine has sunk into a most dissolute life, more so than is known to any of my own acquaintances, even in their least-attractive pursuits. I want to find this young man, and attempt to reconcile him with his father." He looked a little self-conscious, perhaps aware of how slender his chances were. "I have given my word, but I do not know where to begin. I was hoping that Hester might know at least the areas where I could start. He is apparently concerned with a deeper level of vice than mere gambling, drinking, or the use of prostitutes."

Squeaky felt a sharp stab of alarm. This sounded like a story of grief that Hester would get caught up in much too much. Next thing you know, she'd be helping him, making inquiries herself. What really worried Squeaky was not just the harm she could come to, but the ugly things about his own past that she might learn. As it was, she might guess, but there was a great deal about himself that he had managed to keep from her, in fact to even pretty well wipe out of his own memory.

"I can help you," he said quietly, his heart thumping in his chest so violently he feared it made his body shake. "I'd be the one she'd ask anyway. I know that kind o' thing. Some things a lady doesn't need to find out about, even if she has nursed soldiers an' the like."

Henry Rathbone smiled very slightly. "That would be good of you, sir. I'm afraid I don't know your name."

"Robinson. Most folks call me Squeaky." He felt faintly embarrassed explaining it, but no one ever used his given name. He had practically forgotten the sound of it himself, nor did he care for it. "I'd be happy to oblige. Tell me what you need, an' I'll make a few inquiries as to where you can begin."

❖

*W*hen Henry Rathbone had gone, Squeaky closed his account books, which were perfectly up-to-date anyway. He locked them back in the cupboard in his office where he kept them, and went to look for Hester.

He found her upstairs. Her long, white apron was blood-spattered, and as usual, her hair poked out where she had pinned it back too tightly and it had worked its way undone. She looked up from the clean surgical instruments she was putting back in their cases.

"Yes, Squeaky? What is it?"

His mind was already made up. She must not have any idea what he intended, or, for that matter, that Henry Rathbone had called to see her. Hester was clever, so he would need to lie very well indeed for her to believe him. In fact it might be better not to hide the fact that he was lying, but just to fool her as to which lie it was.

"I need to go away for a little while, not quite sure how long," he began.

She looked at him coolly, her blue-gray eyes seeming to bore right into his head.

"Then we shall have to manage without you," she said calmly. "We are well up-to-date with most things. I'm sure Claudine and I will be able to take care of the money and the shopping between us."

Squeaky wondered why she did not ask where he was going, and what for. Was it because she had already decided that she knew? Well, she didn't!

"A friend of mine is in trouble," he started to explain. "His son has gone missing and he's afraid he's in danger." There now, that was the truth—almost.

A momentary sympathy touched her face, and then vanished.

"Really? I'm sorry."

She didn't believe him! That hurt, particularly because Squeaky was doing this just to protect Hester from herself. He knew the kind of place Lucien Wentworth was likely to have ended up in, and that was a part of the underworld that even Hester didn't imagine, for all her experience. This was all his own fault. He had broken the first rule of successful lying—never answer questions that people hadn't asked you!

"It's Christmas," he said, as if that explained everything.

She smiled with extraordinary sweetness, which made him feel worse.

"Then go and help him, Squeaky. But remember to come back. We should miss you very badly if you didn't."

"It's . . ." he began. How could he explain it to her without her wanting to help? And she couldn't. It was a dark world she shouldn't ever have to know about. Weren't war and disease enough without her seeing all about depravity as well?

She was waiting.

"It's my home here," he said abruptly. "Of course I'll be back!" Then he turned and walked away, furious with himself for his total incompetence. All this respectability had rotted his brain. He couldn't even tell an efficient lie anymore.

Downstairs and outside he caught a hansom south toward the river. He begrudged the expense, but there was no time to waste with buses, changing from one to another, and even then not ending up where you really wanted to be.

It might take him some time to find Crow, the man whose help he needed. Crow had intended to be a doctor, but various circumstances, mostly financial but not entirely, had cut short his studies. Squeaky had considered it indelicate to ask what those circumstances were, and he had no need to know. As it was, Crow's medical knowledge was sufficient for him to practice, unofficially, among the poor and frequently semi-criminal who thronged the docksides both north and south of the river around the Pool of London. He took his payment in whatever form was offered: food, clothes, sometimes services, sometimes a promise both parties knew could not be kept. Crow never referred to such debts again.

It took Squeaky the rest of the afternoon, a conversational supper of pork pie at The Goat and Compasses, and then more walking and questioning, to find Crow in a tenement house just short of the Shadwell Docks. Since he wanted a favor, Squeaky waited until Crow had seen his patient and collected his fee of sixpence—which was insisted upon by the patient's father—and the two of them were free to walk out onto the road beside the river.

Crow turned up the collar of his long, black coat and pulled it more tightly around himself against the icy wind coming up off the water. He was tall—several inches taller than Squeaky—and at least twenty-five years younger. Today he had a hat jammed over his long straight black hair, but in the lamplight Squeaky saw the same wide smile on his face as usual. He seemed to have too many teeth, fine and strong.

"You must want something very badly," he remarked, looking sideways at Squeaky. "And it isn't a doctor. You've got plenty of those much nearer Portpool Lane. You look agitated."

"I *am* agitated," Squeaky snapped. He told Crow about Henry Rathbone's visit to the clinic and his request for help in finding Lucien Wentworth. As they strode in the dark along the narrow street in the ice-flecked bitter wind, the cobbles slick under their feet, he also told him about the sort of indulgence that Lucien Wentworth had apparently sunk into.

Crow shook his head. "You can't let Hester go looking into that!" he said anxiously. "Don't even imagine it."

"I'm not!" Squeaky was disgusted, and hurt. Crow should have known him better than to even have thought such a thing. "Why do you think I'm looking for you, you fool?"

Crow stopped in his tracks. "Me? I don't know places like that. I've treated a few opium addicts, but for other things—slashes, broken bones, not the opium. As far as I know, there isn't anything you can do for it."

Squeaky felt a wash of panic rise inside him. He couldn't do this alone. He knew enough about the underworld of self-indulgence to be aware of its labyrinthine depths and dangers. What on earth had possessed him to begin this? He should have told Henry Rathbone that the whole thing was impossible. For that matter, Rathbone should have told Lucien's father that in the first place. Squeaky was really losing his grip. Respectability was an idiot's calling.

"Right!" he said tartly. "I'll go back and tell Hester I can't do it."

"You didn't tell her anything about it in the first place," Crow pointed out, but there was no smile in his eyes.

"And how do I tell Mr. Rathbone that I can't do it?" Squeaky said sarcastically. "Without her knowing, eh? She's clever, that one. She can read a lie like it was writ on your face. She'll know, whatever I say."

Crow thrust his hands into his pockets. His hands always seemed to be bare, whatever the weather. Squeaky looked at him. "Why don't you get someone to pay you with a pair o' gloves?" he said pointedly.

Crow ignored the remark. "Are you saying obliquely that you will tell Hester I refused to help?"

"Obliquely? Obliquely? You mean sideways?" Squeaky said crossly. "Why can't you say it straight out? And no, I'm not saying it sideways, I'm telling you plain that she'll know, 'cause if she were in my place, you'd be the person she'd ask. Which comes to my point. You want me to tell her you won't help, or you want to tell her yourself?"

Crow shook his head. "You haven't lost your touch, Squeaky. You're a hard man."

"Thank you," Squeaky said with unexpected appreciation.

Crow glared at him. "It wasn't a compliment! What do we know about this Lucien Wentworth, apart from the fact that his father is wealthy and seems to have let him have a lot more money than is good for him?"

Squeaky shrugged and started to walk again, talking half over his shoulder as Crow caught up with him. He repeated what Henry Rathbone had told him about Lucien's weakness for physical pleasure, his need to feel a sense of power, to feel admired, to feel—as it might appear to his deluded and immature mind—loved.

Behind them a string of barges went downriver with the ebbing tide, their riding lights bright sparks in the wind and darkness. To the south a foghorn sounded mournfully.

Crow's expression grew grimmer as he tramped beside Squeaky. Finally they turned inland and slightly up the slope, leaving the sounds of the water behind them. The thickening gloom of the winter night lay ahead. Lamps shone one after another along the narrow street, angular beacons toward the busier High Street.

"It's going to be a long night," Crow said as they reached the crossroad. They waited for the traffic to clear, and then hurried over, their boots splashing in the gutter and then crunching on the cobbles already slicked with ice. "And we may not find anything."

Squeaky wanted to tell him to stop complaining, but he knew that Crow was right, so he said nothing for several minutes.

"Let's have a drink first," he suggested finally. He thought of offering to pay for both of them, but that was a bad habit to start.

*I*t was, as Crow had said, a very long night. They began with extremely discreet inquiries in the Haymarket. The area was notorious for the prostitutes who patrolled its pavements so openly that no decent woman went there, even if accompanied by her husband. However well-dressed she was, she would be likely to be taken for a lady of the night. In this area such women might be indistinguishable from ladies of society, especially those whose taste was a little daring.

"I don't know what we'll learn here," Crow said, watching a couple of young women quite openly sidle up to a group of theatergoers.

"Do you know which theaters are fashionable right now for tastes a bit sharper than usual?" Squeaky asked challengingly.

"My patients don't come up this way," Crow admitted. "East End music halls are more their line, if they've a few pence to spare."

"Then shut up, and watch," Squeaky retorted. "And follow me."

They tried to find places selling more than alcohol, entertainment, and the chance to pick up a prostitute.

Their first three attempts were abortive, but the fourth led them to a very small theater off Piccadilly where the drama on stage was overshadowed by the exchanges in the many private boxes and on the narrow stairs. The lighting was yellow and very dim, making most of the people look sallow and a little sinister. Heaven only knew what they looked like in daylight.

Squeaky watched and waited. He did not know the names of the current young dandies who indulged themselves. Their dull eyes were half-focused, lids drooping. Opium, he thought to himself.

He studied one young man closely, and, brushing past him, felt the quality of the cloth in his jacket sleeve. Yes, definitely money there. He hoped he had not lost his childhood art of picking pockets. There was often very good information to be had from the contents of a gentleman's pocket—his name and address from his card, if nothing else.

Squeaky knew that moving unnoticed in places such as these would require a little money, and he had no intention whatsoever of financing it himself. His money was earned with proper work these days, and deserved to be spent respectably. Better to pick pockets without Crow's noticing, though. You never knew what his peculiar aversions might be. There was no accounting for taste, or superstition.

From that theater they learned of others, more daring. The first cost them even to gain entrance.

From the outside it looked like a perfectly ordinary public house.

"Don't look worth the trouble," Squeaky said disparagingly, regarding the chipped pillars and peeling plaster with distaste.

"An affectation, perhaps?" Crow suggested. Then he hurried over to explain. "A suggestion to the eye of the more sordid appetites catered to within?"

Squeaky was amused, not so much by the idea as by the wording Crow chose. He shrugged and paid for their entry.

"Ye're right," he said generously as soon as they were through the archway and down the steps into the main room. It was crowded with people, all of them with glasses or goblets in their hands, except the two almost-naked women who were practicing the most extraordinary and vulgar contortions on a makeshift stage, to the hoots and jeers of the onlookers.

"They'll be needing me professionally," Crow observed, wincing at a particularly unnatural-looking move.

Squeaky made no comment. He began to methodically talk to one person after another, asking questions, learning little.

It took them over an hour to learn that Lucien was known here, but had not been seen in more than a month.

They moved on to another place where they learned nothing, and then a farther tavern that at first seemed very helpful. However, in the end the man they found there turned out not to be Lucien, merely some other lost youth bent on finding oblivion.

By four in the morning Squeaky was tired and cold. His head ached. And his feet were sore. He realized all the reasons he had been willing to give up the pursuit of temporary pleasure in favor of a warm bed in the Portpool Lane clinic, and only the very occasional night awake chasing around after other people's needs. Even then, his time was not spent outside in the rain and the freezing wind, with his feet wet and water sliding down his neck from the rain. Being inside a low-ceilinged room and among the confusion of loud voices was not much better. He had forgotten how he disliked stupid laughter and the crush of bodies in narrow spaces, the smell of stale smoke and drink. Even the music had less appeal than it used to.

They entered a cellar deep below a tavern. The yellow gaslight made the stone walls look even more pitted and stained. They did at least serve good brandy. Apart from warming Squeaky's body a bit, the drink encouraged him to think that this was the kind of place that might attract a man like Lucien Wentworth, who was raised to know the quality of brandy and partook only of the best.

It was actually Crow who began the conversation with a nearby stranger that finally yielded the first scent of Lucien.

"Clever," Crow observed amiably to the man nearest him. They were both looking at a provocatively dressed young woman who was miming an obscene joke to the delight of onlookers.

"Cost yer," the young man remarked. "But they all do."

"I prefer something a bit . . ." Crow hesitated. "Unusual."

The young man looked him up and down as if assessing his taste. "You'da liked Sadie." He sighed wistfully. He was so slight as to be almost emaciated. The bones of his wrists looked fragile when his shirtsleeves slid back. "She was beautiful."

"Really . . ." Crow had difficulty pretending interest. Squeaky realized he had no idea what kind of woman Crow liked. The subject had never arisen.

"Face pale as a lily," the young man went on dreamily. "Hair like black silk. And sea-blue eyes, bright as deep water in the sun."

Squeaky let his mind wander. This was all a waste of time.

Crow was still pretending to be interested. "She sounds different," he said, regarding the young man closely. You pursued her? Was she all you imagined?"

The young man lifted one bony shoulder. "No idea. She only had time for Lucien."

That caught Squeaky's attention, and he sat up-right too quickly. The young man turned to stare at him, breaking the thread of his remembrance.

Crow glared at Squeaky.

Squeaky scratched himself, as if it had been a sudden itch that had disturbed him. "Too bad," he commiserated. He caught Crow's eye and decided to say no more.

"Is she still around here?" Crow asked casually.

"What?"

"The girl with the sea-blue eyes."

"Oh, Sadie? Haven't seen her." The young man

fished in his pocket, but apparently did not find what he was looking for. He furrowed his brow. "I'm getting out of here. This is becoming tedious. Do you want to come to Potter's with me?"

"Sounds like a good idea," Crow agreed, without asking Squeaky. "I'd like to hear more about Sadie. You make her sound special, something new."

"Won't do you any good." The young man rose to his feet, and swayed a little. Crow caught him by the arm, steadying him. "Obliged," the young man acknowledged the assistance, letting out a belch of alcoholic fumes. Don't bother with Sadie. I told you, she went with Lucien."

"Where to?" Crow asked him, still holding his arm.

"God knows." The young man waved a hand in the air.

"We aren't on conversational terms with God," Squeaky put in acidly. "I ask, but he doesn't bleedin' answer."

The young man started to laugh and ended with a hacking cough.

Crow patted him on the back. It was a useless gesture, but one that allowed him to keep a firm hold on his arm and prevent him from collapsing altogether as he guided him toward the way out.

The journey to Potter's was made erratically along footpaths slick with ice. Holding on to each other was a way to maintain balance as well as to make sure that they did not lose the young man, and that he did not pass out in one of the many doorways. He might well freeze to death if he did.

"Fool," Squeaky muttered under his breath. Now that he was not making money out of other people's vices, he had a far less tolerant view of them. "Fool!" he repeated as the young man stumbled. He would have fallen flat on the ice-covered paving stones if Crow and Squeaky had not yanked him to his feet again.

When they finally reached Potter's they found that the place was dimly lit, mostly by tallow candles in a variety of holders. Despite the lateness of the hour it was still full of people. Some were drinking, while others lounged in corners quietly smoking what Squeaky knew from past experience was tobacco liberally laced with other substances, possibly opium derivatives of some sort. The air was heavy and rancid with the stench of smoke, alcohol, sweat, and various other bodily odors.

Crow wrinkled his nose and shot a grim look

at Squeaky. Squeaky tried to smile but knew it looked sickly on his face.

They were offered brandy, and bought some to try to revive the young man. He seemed to be falling asleep, or possibly into a kind of stupor.

The sharp spirit going down his throat stirred him, at least temporarily. "What?" he said abruptly. "What did you say?"

"You were telling us about Sadie," Crow prompted him. "How beautiful she was, and how much fun."

"Yes, Sadie." He repeated the name as if rolling the flavor around his mouth. "What a woman. Skin like . . . like . . ." He could not think of anything adequate. "So alive," he said instead. "Always laughing, dancing, making jokes, kissing someone outrageously, places you wouldn't believe."

"Lucien . . ." Crow put in.

"Oh yes, him especially," the young man agreed. "He would do anything for her, and did." A slow, dreamy smile spread across his face. "She dared him to swallow a live fish . . . eel, I think it was. Revolting."

"Did he?" Squeaky asked.

The young man looked at him with disgust. "Of

course he did. Told you, he'd do anything for her. Admired her." There was envy in his face. "Said she made him feel like a god—or a fallen angel, maybe. Can you see it?" He smiled a little vacantly. "Spiraling down from the lip of heaven in an everlasting descent to the fires of hell and the dark underlight of those who have tasted all that there is and know everything that the universe can hold." He began to laugh. It was a strange, shrill sound broken by hiccups.

One of the candles on the cellar wall guttered and went out.

There were several moments of silence before he spoke again. "And of course there was Niccolo," he added. "Never knew if she actually wanted him, or if she just used him to make Lucien mad with jealousy. Either way, it worked."

"Niccolo?" Crow repeated the name. "What was he like? Who was he?"

The young man stared blankly.

"Who was he?" Crow repeated with exaggerated patience.

"No idea." The young man seemed to lose interest. Squeaky fetched more brandy, but it didn't help. Their informant was beginning to drift off into a stupor.

"Who was Niccolo?" Squeaky said, his voice edged with threat.

The young man stared at him and blinked. "Sadie's lover," he replied, giggling in a falsetto voice. "Sadie's other lover." He started to laugh again, then slowly slid off the chair and fell in a heap on the floor.

Crow bent down as if to pick him up, or at least to try.

"Leave him," Squeaky ordered. "He's probably as well off there as anywhere else. You won't get anything more out of him. We need to find this Sadie. Can't be too many as look like her. C'mon."

It was now past five in the morning, and there was hardly anyone left sober enough to give them any answers. They went out into the early morning darkness and the bleak easterly wind. Crow started to turn down toward the river, and his home.

"No yer don't!" Squeaky said sharply. "We in't finished yet."

Crow snatched his arm away. "There's nobody else awake at this hour, you fool!" he said impatiently. "It's pointless looking now. Not that there's much point at any time. I want some breakfast, then to sleep."

"So do I. Come to the clinic and we'll get both."

"Yes? And how are you going to explain all this to Hester?" Crow asked witheringly.

"I'm not." Squeaky was disgusted with Crow's lack of imagination. "I'm not going to tell her anything. We'll get a good breakfast, then find a couple of rooms there with no one in them, and she won't know." Then another thought occurred to him. "It's warm there, and only a mile away."

Crow gave in, pretending it was a favor to Squeaky. Then he gave one of his flashing grins, which was a mark of his good nature and slightly eccentric sense of humor. "Come on then. I suppose it's really not a bad place at all."

❖

The following evening was much easier. They now knew exactly who they were looking for. Additionally, contacts whom Squeaky had used in the past could be persuaded to yield a little information in return for promises of unquestioning medical help for things, such as unexplained knife wounds or even the odd gunshot.

Sadie's name was recognized by several people they asked in taverns and small theaters of the more louche kind. It seemed she was as great a beauty as the young man the previous evening had suggested, although she did not apparently sing or dance. But, far more arresting than mere physical perfection, she was said to possess a wild energy, imagination, and laughter that fascinated more men than just Lucien Wentworth, although they all seemed agreed that he was the most obsessed with her. He had already come close to killing a man who had tried to claim her forcibly.

"At each other's throats over 'er, they were," one raddled old woman told them, where they found her in a busy and very expensive brothel off Half Moon Street. "Stuck a knife in 'is guts, that Lucien did. Daft bastard." She sucked at her few teeth where the taste of whisky still lingered. 'E'll kill somebody one day. If 'e din't already."

Squeaky silently provided some more.

"Ta'," she said, grasping hold of it with gnarled hands, lumpy and disfigured by gout. "Ever seen dogs fight? Like that, it was. Sneerin' an' teasin' at each other. An' she loved it. Food an' drink it were to 'er. The sight o' blood fair drove 'er wild. Eyes bright as a madwoman, and a glow on 'er skin like she were lit up inside."

"Where is she now?" Crow asked her, controlling his voice with difficulty.

"Dunno." She shook her head.

"Did the man live?" he asked. "The one Lucien knifed?"

"Never 'eard," she said with a shrug. "Prob'ly."

Squeaky looked at the swollen hands. "Where'd he go, this Lucien?" He tried to imagine the pain. He reached out and put his thin, strong fingers over hers. "I s'pect you know, if you think about it," he suggested.

"No I don't," she told him. "Places best not talked about. I don't know nothing." She nodded. "Safer that way."

"Wise to be careful who you talk to," Squeaky agreed. "Best if you just talk to me, an' him." He nodded toward Crow. Then very slowly he tightened his grip on her hand, squeezing the swollen joints.

She let out a shriek of pain. Her lips drew back in fury, showing stumps of teeth.

"Oh, how careless of me," Squeaky said in mock surprise. "Gout, is it? Very painful. So they say. You'll have to leave off the strong drink. Where did you say they went, then? I didn't hear you right." He allowed his hand to tighten just a fraction.

She let out a string of abuse that should have curdled the wine, but she also named a couple of public houses. One was off an alley to the south of Oxford Street, and the other to the north, in a tiny square behind Wigmore Street.

She looked at him with venom. "They'll eat you alive, they will. Go on, then, I dare yer! Think yer know it all? East End scum, y'are. Know nothing. East End's kid's stuff, all there up front. West End's different. They'll drown yer, an' walk away whistlin'. Find yer body in the gutter next mornin', an' nobody'll give a toss. Nobody'll dare ter."

"She's right," Crow said warningly as they went outside again into the icy street.

"An' what do you know about the West End?" Squeaky dismissed him.

Crow blinked. For a moment Squeaky thought he saw something quite different in the blue eyes, as if he had once been the sort of man who knew such places. Then the idea seemed absurd, and Crow was just the same amiable "would-be" doctor he'd known for years.

"We better tell Mr. Rathbone that we can't find

what happened to Lucien Wentworth," Squeaky said aloud. "He could've gone anywhere—Paris even, or Rome."

"There's no need to give up," Crow argued. "We've a fair chance of finding him."

"Course we have!" Squeaky responded. "An' what damn good will that be? Best if his father never hears the kind o' company he kept. If he went to these places—an' I have heard of them, no matter what you think—then he isn't coming back. They don't need to know that."

Crow was silent for several moments. "Is that what you would want?" he said finally.

Squeaky was indignant. "How the hell do I know? As if I had children what should've been gentlemen."

"I think we should tell them the truth," Crow replied thoughtfully. "At least tell Mr. Rathbone the truth. Let him decide what to tell Lucien's father."

"Soft as muck, you are!" Squeaky shook his head. "And about as much use. What'll he want to know that for? Tell him Lucien's gone to Paris, and he'll stop looking."

"Then don't tell him," Crow replied. "I will."

*L*ate in the afternoon, only eight days before Christmas now, Squeaky and Crow together alighted from the hansom cab on Primrose Hill. They walked by the light of the street lamp across the pavement and up the path to Henry Rathbone's house. It had taken a certain amount of inquiring to find out where he lived, and they were later than they had intended to be. Squeaky felt nervous, and—in spite of the fact that Crow hid it well—he knew that he did too. This was a quiet neighborhood and eminently respectable. They were both ill-fitting strangers here. Added to that, they carried with them news that would not be welcome. It was really a message of defeat.

Squeaky hesitated with his hand on the brass knocker. He was furious with himself for being such a coward. He had never been in awe of anyone when he was a businessman, selling women to those who wanted or needed to buy. He had despised them and was perfectly happy that they should know it. It was a straight exchange: money for the use of a woman.

Well, maybe it was not quite that simple, but

close enough. There were never any questions of honor or embarrassment in it. Violence, now and again, of course. People needed to be kept to their side of the arrangement. They tended to slip out of it if you allowed them to. Let yourself be taken advantage of once and it would happen again and again.

"Are you going to knock, or stand there holding that thing?" Crow asked peevishly.

Squeaky picked it up and let it fall with a hard bang.

"Now look what you made me do!" he accused, turning to glare at Crow.

The door swung open, revealing a calm-faced butler.

"Good afternoon, gentlemen. How may I be of service to you?"

Squeaky swallowed and nearly choked.

"We would like to speak to Mr. Henry Rathbone, if you please," Crow answered, while Squeaky tried to collect himself and regain his composure.

The butler blinked and looked confused.

"Mr. Rathbone asked Mr. Robinson here to perform a service for him," Crow continued. "We have come to report our findings so far, and see what Mr. Rathbone would like us to do next."

"Indeed?"

The butler still seemed uncomfortable. It was hardly surprising. Squeaky was lean and snaggle-toothed, and had long gray hair falling onto his collar. Crow had a charming smile with far too many teeth. His hair was black as soot, as was his bedraggled coat with its flapping tails. And— simply because he had had no time to return home and put it down—he still had his doctor's Glad-stone bag with him.

Squeaky drew in his breath to try a better ex-planation.

Perhaps because of the length of time they had been on the step, Henry Rathbone appeared in the hall behind the butler. He recognized Squeaky im-mediately.

"Ah, Mr. Robinson. You have some news?" He looked at Crow. "I am afraid I do not know you, sir, but if you are a friend of Mr. Robinson, then you are welcome."

"Crow. Doctor, or almost," Crow said a little sheepishly. There was a note of longing in his voice, as if the "almost" had cost him more than he wanted to admit.

"Henry Rathbone. How do you do, sir? Please come inside. Have you eaten? If not, I can offer you toast, a very agreeable Belgian pâté, or Brie, and perhaps some apple tart and cream. Hot or cold, as you prefer."

Crow could not keep the smile from lighting his face.

Squeaky wanted that supper so badly he could taste it in his mouth already. Guilt at the news he brought overwhelmed him, but only for a couple of seconds.

"Thank you, Mr. Rathbone," he replied quickly, just in case Crow had any other ideas. "That would be very nice indeed." He took a step forward into the hall as the butler pulled the door wider to let him pass.

They sat next to the fire in the sitting room. Squeaky was fascinated first by the number of books in the cases in the walls, and then by the delicate beauty of the two small paintings hung over the mantel. Both were seascapes with an almost luminous quality to the water. He felt Rathbone's eyes on him as he stared, and then the heat of embarrassment burned up his face.

"Boningtons," Henry said quietly. "They've always held a particular appeal for me. I'm glad you like them."

"Yes." Squeaky had no idea what else to say. He

was even more out of his depth than he had expected to be, and it made him highly uncomfortable. Suddenly he did not know what to do with
his hands, or feet.

Crow cleared his throat and stared at Squeaky.

Henry looked at him, waiting.

Squeaky plunged in. Better to get it over with.
"Thing is," he began tentatively. "Thing is . . . we
found word of Mr. Wentworth."

Henry leaned forward eagerly. "You did?
Already? That's a most excellent start."

Squeaky felt the sweat prickle on his skin. He
was making a complete pig's ear of this. He didn't
even mean to be deceptive, except for the best of
reasons, and here he was doing it. Respectability
had put him out of practice of saying anything the
way he meant it.

"Thing is," he began again. "His father's right,
he's picked up with some very bad company indeed. Woman called Sadie, a real bad lot. Seems
he's lost his wits over her. Got tangled up with
a rival, and now there in't anything daft enough
or bad enough he won't do to impress her. Even
damn near killed someone."

He drew in a deep breath. "Mr. Rathbone, he
in't going to come back as long as she'll give 'im

the sort of attention he wants, an' she's playin' him off against this other young fool, clear as day to anyone with eyes in their heads. It's a world you don't know, sir, an' don't want to."

Henry looked sad, but not surprised. "I see," he said quietly. "It seems to be as bad as his father feared." He looked across at Crow. "Do I assume that you agree, Doctor?"

Crow blushed, not for the question, but for the courtesy title to which he had no right. He faced him squarely. "Yes sir. I'm afraid he's sunk to the kind of place people don't come back from. It isn't just the drinking, although that'll get to you in time. It's the violence. It seems this young woman thrives on it. The sight and smell of blood excites her, the idea that men will kill each other over her."

"Are you saying that we shouldn't try?" Henry asked him.

Squeaky drew in his breath to tell him that that was exactly what they were saying, then he saw Crow's face and changed his mind.

"Yes sir," Crow answered gravely. "It's the man's own heart that's keeping him there. I . . . I suppose if we can find him, we could tell him that his father wants him back, but I don't think it'll make any difference. I'd say, sir, that he's best not to know what's become of his son. What he imagines would be bad, but once you've seen something for real, there's no escaping it ever. There's things you don't want to see."

"Lots of things," Henry agreed. "But that is not a reason to turn away. Perhaps if we could persuade Lucien that there is a way back, then . . ."

Squeaky leaned forward. "He doesn't want to come back! There's no one keeping him there except himself. Crow's right, Mr. Rathbone."

"I suppose he is," Henry murmured. "But I have given Mr. Wentworth my promise. If you would be kind enough to tell me the best direction in which to begin, I shall do so. And perhaps any other advice . . ."

Squeaky could not bear it. This man was a babe in the woods. He had not the faintest idea what he was dealing with. He would be robbed and probably killed within the first couple of hours.

"You can't," he said simply. "You'd be done over an' left in the gutter. Maybe even knifed, 'specially if Lucien knows you're after him. I can't let you . . . sir."

"I am not doing it from choice, Mr. Robinson,"

Henry replied gently. "I have promised an old friend that I will do all I can. I have not yet done that. Please, give me whatever advice you have, and allow me to reimburse you for the trouble you have taken so far, and any expense you may have incurred."

"We didn't go to any expense," Squeaky said with an honesty he knew he would regret later. He saw Henry's disbelief in his eyes. "I relieved one or two gentlemen of their wrongful earnings," Squeaky explained without a flicker. "Used 'em to buy a little information. And no trouble neither. So you don't owe us at all." He made to rise to his feet, but Crow did not follow him, so he sat back down again. "And a very good supper too," he added.

Crow took a deep breath, as if to steady himself, then he spoke quickly.

"If you're determined to go an' see for yourself, then I'll come with you. I know the way better than you do."

Squeaky cursed himself. He should have seen that coming. He knew Henry Rathbone was a fool, but he should have realized that Crow was too.

"You neither of you know a damn thing!" he said furiously. "Like sending kittens into a dogfight! I'll come with you." He wanted to add a whole lot more, but there didn't seem to be any point, and every time he opened his mouth he got himself into more trouble.

"Thank you, Mr. Robinson," Henry said with a beautiful smile.

❦

*T*he three of them set out a short while later. This time they took a hansom at Henry Rathbone's expense, and alighted in Oxford Street.

Once they had agreed that they were all going, they had discussed practical plans over tea and fruitcake. Since they were now aware of the kind of woman they were looking for, and her name, as well as that of her other lover, Niccolo, they had clear places to start.

"Off Oxford Street," Squeaky said knowingly. "Nothing cheap. This woman likes money an' class. No fun in getting a couple o' drunkards rolling around on the floor. You can see that any-where."

Henry winced.

Squeaky saw it. "You sure you want to find this Lucien?"

"I am," Henry replied, his voice low.

Crow said nothing, but he was clearly unhappy. He did not argue with Henry. Possibly he even understood, in his own way.

Squeaky rose to his feet. "Then we'll get started."

They went to one public house after another, following the trail of those who had seen or heard of Sadie, or the names Lucien and Niccolo. The songs were ever bawdier as the night went on. In the galleries above the makeshift stages, prostitutes stalked up and down until they attracted the attention of a customer. Then they disappeared into one of the many side rooms provided for the purpose.

There was much drink flowing, mostly whisky and gin. And, with the right request, and accompanied by the right money, laudanum, opium, and various other, stronger substances such as cocaine were available to enhance the vividness of the experience, or to block out a grief that might intrude upon pleasure.

Henry Rathbone masked his distaste, but it was obvious that it was with great difficulty. Then as the evening wore on, Squeaky saw in his eyes a look that he knew was pity.

Crow asked questions, but Squeaky realized how acutely he was watching the people he saw, understanding the pasty skins, the scabs no paint or powder could disguise. A feeling of hopelessness settled over him.

It was near Piccadilly, in a narrow, gaslit old music hall, toward morning, when they met Bessie. She was perhaps fourteen or fifteen. It was hard to tell because she was thin and narrow-chested, but her skin was still blemishless and had some natural color. She was fetching and carrying drinks to people for the barman, who was pouring out and taking money as fast as he could. Bessie wove her way through the crowd with a certain grace, but in spite of her air of innocence, she seemed quite capable of giving back as good as she received in any exchange. One man who ventured to touch her caught a full glass of cider in his lap. He leapt to his feet in fury, to much laughter and jeering from those around him.

"Yer lookin' fer Lucien?" she said in answer to Henry's question. "'E in't 'ere no more. Gone after that Sadie." The expression on her face was not so much disgust as a weary kind of sorrow. "Yer'd think a man like that'd know better, wouldn't yer?"

"You know him?" Henry said quickly.

She shrugged a thin shoulder in an oddly adult gesture. "Talked with 'im some. Listened to 'im, more like. See'd 'ow 'is face lit up when 'e told us about 'er. Think she was like Christmas come. More like bleedin' 'alloween, if you ask me. Let the devils out that night, din't they? God knows wot yer'll meet with." Then her face was wistful. "But she were pretty, in a mad sort o' way."

"Do you know where they went?" Henry asked her. "I am a friend of his father's, and I would dearly like to give him a message."

She shook her head. "I can guess, sort o'," she admitted. "I in't never been there meself, but I 'eard." She hesitated.

"What?" Crow asked quickly.

"I dunno." She snatched the tray on which she carried the glasses and pushed her way back into the crowd.

Crow swore under his breath.

"Do you think she knows something?" Henry asked dubiously. "She's only a child."

Squeaky got up off his seat and forced his way between two men with glasses full of whisky. One slopped over and he swore with low, sustained fury. Squeaky ignored them, and the group of painted women beyond them, flirting desperately. A man and a woman in a red dress argued over the price of opium, another two over cocaine. Squeaky caught up with Bessie again as she neared the barman.

"What were you going to say about Lucien?" he demanded. "You know where we could look." He wondered whether to offer her money, or if it would insult her. She certainly must need it, but those who were the most desperate were also at times the most easily insulted. "We need your help," he finished. If she asked for money, he would give it to her—Henry Rathbone's money, of course.

She looked him up and down, her lips pursed. "'E won't go with yer," she told him.

"I know that," he replied. "But Mr. Rathbone don't. He's . . . a bit innocent, like. He won't stop until he finds out for himself."

Bessie shook her head. "In't goin' ter do any good. But I can 'elp yer, if yer want."

"Show us?"

She hesitated, a flicker of fear crossing her thin, soft face.

"We'll look after yer. Yer won't come to no harm," Squeaky promised rashly, aware even as he said it that he was speaking wildly out of turn.

"I s'pose," she agreed, looking down at the floor, then suddenly up at him, her eyes bright and afraid.

Squeaky cursed to himself. He really was losing his grip.

*O*ver the next two nights Squeaky went with Henry, Crow, and Bessie deeper and deeper into the squalid world of illicit pleasure. In New Bond Street they turned into an alley westward and immediately found themselves on steps down into a garishly lit cellar where both men and women were lying around, some on makeshift beds, others simply on the floor.

Henry stopped a few paces in, his mouth pulled down at the smell.

"Don't stop," Squeaky warned him. "It's opium, an' sweat, an' sex. Don't take no notice."

Henry started moving obediently. A little ahead of them a man in a black coat reeled on wobbly legs, laughing at nothing. To his left someone was weeping; in the red light it was impossible to tell if it was a man or a woman. It was hard for him to think of this as a place of pleasure, and yet these people had come here willingly, at least to begin with.

He watched a man rocking back and forth, his face distorted as in his mind he clung to an ecstasy so brief, so illusory it slipped from him even as they watched.

Bessie led them, occasionally faltering. Often she looked back to make certain they were all there, as if she feared suddenly finding that she was alone, and somehow betrayed. At times she clung to Squeaky, gripping his thin hand so her hard, strong little fingers dug into his flesh. He found it painful, and yet the couple of times she let go, he was hurt, as if she had stopped needing him.

"Squeaky, you're losing your wits," he said to himself with disgust. "You always thought being respectable was stupid. Now you know for certain."

To Henry Rathbone it was a descent into a kind of hell that was not just visual. The noise of it, and the stench of body fluids and stale alcohol were almost worse. His stomach clenched at the sight of ground-in filth mixed with the harsher stench of sewage. Voices were loud, angry, then whining. Ahead of him someone laughed hysterically and without meaning.

To Crow it was a series of sicknesses. A man shambled across the floor with the gait of the drunkard and collapsed sideways. His nose was swollen and broken-veined, the skin of his arms flaccid. Crow recoiled without meaning to, and knocked into another man who turned on him. His face was scabbed and ulcerated, yellowed with jaundice, the whites of his eyes the color of urine.

The nightmare grew worse.

Crow bumped into a couple who seemed to have no control of their limbs, and little awareness of where they were, their eyes vague, unfocused.

The man, no more than thirty years old, reached to grasp a bottle, only to have it slip from his fingers and smash on the floor.

Two old men engaged in disjointed conversation, then became lost, as if the ideas behind it escaped them into the fog.

Crow knew the reasons. He knew that those who drank to oblivion seldom ate. Their bellies were bloated, and yet they were starving. Perhaps that was the core of it all: their dreams and their senses were frantically consuming but never fed.

Then in all the babble and moaning someone

mentioned Lucien's name. Crow spun around. An old woman with unnaturally bright hennaed hair was telling Henry very clearly that she had seen Lucien, only two days ago.

"Pretty, 'e were, an' gentle spoke," she said with a toothless grin. "Twenty years ago, in me prime, I'd 'ave 'ad 'im."

Crow thought her prime was more like forty years ago, or even fifty, but he did not interrupt.

"Who was he with?" Henry asked her patiently.

"Another pretty feller," she replied. "But got a nasty eye. Looked at yer like rats, 'e did. Ol' Roberts 'ates rats. Breaks their necks if he catches 'em." She held up both her hands and twisted them sharply, as if she were wringing the water out of laundry. She made a clicking sound with her tongue, to imitate the breaking of bone.

"Were they friends, these two?" Henry asked her with as much patience as he could manage.

"Nobody's friends." She looked at him witheringly. "Particular these two weren't. After the same bint ter lie with, weren't they!"

"Sadie," he guessed.

"Mebbe. Long-legged piece, with black 'air."

"Where will I find them?" He was blunt at last.

She cackled with laughter.

"Where will I find them?" he repeated, with an edge of annoyance.

She blinked. "Wot?"

"Where are they, yer stupid mare?" Squeaky interrupted angrily.

She turned to him, her eyes suddenly focusing. "Go an' ask Shadow Man," she hissed. "See if 'e'll tell yer. Go an' get 'is soul back fer 'im."

There was a moment's silence. One or two people close to them pulled back a step or two.

"Who is Shadow Man?" Henry asked.

"Shadwell, 'is name is. The devil, I call 'im." She stared at him, then her face seemed to contort into a kind of convulsion, and she started to shiver violently.

Henry turned to Crow. "Can you help her, man? She's having some kind of a fit. Can't you . . ." His voice trailed off.

"No one can help her," Crow answered. "Her demons are inside her own head. Come on. We've one more place to try tonight. It's not far from here."

"Are you sure?"

"Had enough?" Crow looked at him with some sympathy.

Henry lifted his chin a little. "No. If we've more

to try, then we'll try them. Word is bound to spread. How much deeper is there to go?"

"There are tunnels under the river," Squeaky answered. "Old ones, before they rebuilt the sewers. Believe me, we're not at the bottom yet. Although the real bottom may be up a bit from there."

Henry stared at him, confused.

"There's a bottom of despair," Squeaky replied. "And a bottom of power, an' cruelty. We haven't even touched the places where people do things to each other like some of those paintings by that German feller, or Dutch he was maybe. Pictures of torture, an' things with animals you wouldn't even think of."

"Lucien wouldn't . . ." Henry began, then stopped. "Or perhaps he would. As you said, the real demons are in your own mind. If they conquer, perhaps anything of other people's pain may be illusory to you."

Squeaky was not certain what he meant. The demons he knew were real enough: cold, hunger, disease, fear, and even at times loneliness. That wasn't illusory.

"Who's this Shadwell?" Crow asked, looking at each of them in turn. "Do you think that's just the drink talking in her?"

"No," Bessie interrupted them for the first time, shaking her head violently. "'E's real."

"Have you seen him?" Henry asked her.

She put her hands up to her face, her eyes wide with fear. "No! I don't look. But I 'eard. 'Is voice is soft, like 'e got summink in 'is throat an' 'e can't speak proper. But you can 'ear 'im anyway."

Squeaky looked sideways at her. "Yer sure you ain't making that up?"

"Course I'm sure! 'E's real! I'll show yer where 'e's bin, but I won't take yer there." She put out her hand, and—cursing himself again—he took it.

She led them through freezing alleys. The steady dripping of eaves left long icicles hanging like glittering daggers above them in the sporadic lamplight. The air was bitter with the acrid smell of old chimneys and open drains.

They turned into a tiny square and through an archway into a whorehouse. The madame eyed them grimly.

"I apologize," Henry said hastily. "We appear to be lost."

The woman let out a gale of laughter, and belched from the depths of her huge stomach. "Yer got no money, get out. That way!" She jabbed her fingers to the left.

They escaped obediently down steps, along a somber passage and up again into a noisy hall that was apparently the entrance to a very large house. It was initially quiet, except for a sudden shout that made them all start and then move closer together, as if in the face of some unseen threat.

A man appeared in the doorway, leaning on a stick to support himself. He was Squeaky's height, but skeletally thin. His face was pale, as if it were painted with white lead, and his eyes were odd colors, one lighter than the other, and both ringed with black. He was dressed in old-fashioned breeches to the knee and a velvet frock coat, all in a faded lavender. He could have stepped out of a previous century. He surveyed them.

"Nothing for you here," he said, pronouncing his words with pedantic care. "Trying to get lost, are you?" He addressed the question to Henry Rathbone.

"We are looking for a friend," Henry replied, matching courtesy for courtesy. "We think he may have come this way, and perhaps you have seen him?"

"I see everyone, my dear." The man took a step closer, and Squeaky was aware of a draft of cold air in the room. "Sooner or later," the man added with a twitch of his lips that was not quite a smile. "What does your friend look like?"

"In his early thirties, dark-haired, slender, unusually handsome." Henry struggled to think of something unique about Lucien. "His eyes are actually dark hazel, not brown, and he speaks with a slightly husky voice." Was he making a fool of himself, by being so detailed? What would this odd-looking man notice about anyone else's appearance?

"Oh, yes," the man said with a sigh as if some deep emotion filled him. "He came this way, with Sadie, of course, with dear, fickle, dangerous Sadie. Such fun, on her good days. Or perhaps one should say 'nights.' Cruel sometimes, but then aren't we all?" He looked directly at Bessie, who shivered and stepped backward, closer to Squeaky.

Without thinking, Squeaky put his arm around her, and then wondered what on earth he was doing. He was going soft! His emotions were rotting along with his wits.

"Where can we find them?" Henry asked, still facing the man in his absurd lavender velvet. Squeaky marveled at his persistence. If he was afraid, there was nothing of it in his face, his calm blue eyes. Only looking at his hands did he see that they were stiff, as though he had to concentrate to keep them hanging at his sides, apparently casually. What a strange man he was, completely incomprehensible. Squeaky wanted to despise him—and yet he found that he could not.

This whole adventure was a very bad idea. He should have had more sense, and sent Henry Rathbone and his dreams on his way. That would have been best for everyone—even this spoiled, self-indulgent young man in his descent to hell. Let him go, if that was what he wanted. He wasn't coming back; anyone but a fool knew that.

The lavender-coated man turned slowly on his heel, keeping his balance with difficulty, and pointed to a small door to his left. "That way," he whispered. "And down, always down."

"Thank you, Mr. . . ." Henry said.

"Ash," the man replied with a bow. "Lionel Ash."

"Thank you, Mr. Ash."

Crow went first. They had opened the door, and were through it before Mr. Ash called after them. "Be careful of the blood! Don't slip on it."

Crow froze.

Henry turned back. "What blood?" he said grimly, a flicker of annoyance in his face.

"At the bottom of the stairs," Mr. Ash answered. "On the floor. Terrible mess."

"Whose blood?" Squeaky lunged toward Ash and gripped him by the throat, his strong fingers pressing into the scrawny, completely unresisting flesh.

"My, haven't we got a nasty temper!" Ash said, seeming quite unaffected by having his neck squeezed till Squeaky could feel the sinews and the bones of his spine. Squeaky tried to yank Ash off his feet, and found him unaccountably heavy.

"Whose blood?" he hissed.

"Why, the ones who were killed there, stupid!" Ash answered. "Heartless, it was." He gave a violent shudder, as if he were seized with some kind of convulsion. Then, just as quickly, he went completely limp. Suddenly he seemed to collapse and tears streamed down his white cheeks. "So much blood," he whispered. "So much."

Crow swore under his breath. He glanced at Bessie, then at Henry Rathbone, his brow furrowed.

"You had better let him go," he advised Squeaky,

nodding toward Ash in his ridiculous lavender coat. "He can't tell us anything if he can't breathe."

Squeaky loosened his grip, then pushed Ash hard against the wall. "Who was killed?" he said between his teeth.

Ash straightened his velvet coat. His eyes were narrow, like slits in the paper-white of his face.

"The handsome young man, and the woman with so much black hair," he replied. "Isn't that who you were looking for?"

Henry's shoulders sagged, and the anger and hope drained out of his eyes. "You said he'd gone down." He shook his head.

"Oh yes, far, far down, places most people don't even know about," Ash agreed. "Dream, maybe, in the silent reaches of the night, and wake up sick with a cold sweat. Down there where the shadows move in shadows!" He gave a little giggle that was almost a sob. "Shadow Man."

Suddenly Henry was angry. "Your nightmares are no more real than any other drunkard's or opium addict's. They're paper devils of your own making. Is Lucien alive or dead?"

"A good philosophical question." Ash's attention was now completely focused on Henry, as though Crow and Squeaky were not real, and

67

Bessie was half a creature of this world anyway. "At what point do we step across that slender, eternal line, eh?"

"When our hearts stop beating and our eyes cloud over," Henry snapped.

"Ah—hearts." More tears slid down Ash's face. "Who knows where their hearts are, or ever were? Eyes can be cloudy in more ways than one. Who sees? Who doesn't?"

Squeaky was losing his patience again. He grasped Ash by the collar of his velvet coat and jerked him around. "I think we'd better take him with us," he said to Henry. "He's a bit slow to give a straight answer." He yanked him a couple of steps farther toward the door, and the collar of his velvet jacket tore, leaving the lapels crooked and a rent down the collar's back seam.

Ash's face contorted with fury. It was still totally colorless because of the strange cosmetic he had smeared over it, but his dark lips were pulled back from small teeth, yellow and sharp. "You'll pay for that!" he snarled. "You Philistine! You sniveling animal! Go find your Lucien." He jabbed long-nailed fingers toward the door. "And be careful he doesn't tear your heart out, too!"

Crow slammed the door open and grabbed

Bessie by the hand. Squeaky followed them onto a short landing, Henry behind them, then down the narrow stone steps. There was a faint light from a lantern on the wall, and at the bottom, where it widened by several feet, there were dark stains. It was impossible by the look of them to know what they were, but in his mind he had no doubt that they were human blood.

Henry stood still, regarding the silent stone walls and floor, breathing in the stale smells: mud, candle tallow, something metallic, a sourness like body waste, old terror, and despair.

"Was Lucien the victim, or did he kill Niccolo and Sadie here?" His voice shook a little. He was giving words to his own worst fear, and Squeaky knew it as certainly as if he had known the man for years. He did not want to know him. He did not want to be forced into liking him, even admiring him. Rathbone was a dreamer and a fool. He had no grip on the realities of the world at all. He was like some child—far more so than Bessie, who at least knew what to expect of life.

Squeaky wanted to say something clever, but knew that whatever he said had to be the truth. He looked at Crow, but Crow was inspecting the floor and the lower parts of the walls. There appeared to be scratches on the stone and spatters of blood—if it was blood. Somebody had been horribly injured here—probably bled to death. Who had moved the body, and why?

"Are you sure you want to do this?" Crow turned to Henry. "If it was Lucien who was killed here, his father isn't going to want to hear that. If it was he who killed Niccolo or Sadie, he's going to want to hear that even less. Wouldn't you rather just tell him we tried, but we lost the trail? He doesn't need to know different."

"Of course I'd rather tell him that," Henry said quietly. His eyes stared into the darkness ahead of them, where the passageway seemed to go upward again, but at a slope rather than by steps. "But I'm not a very good liar."

"Then I'll do it for you," Squeaky offered. "I'm excellent."

Henry laughed quietly. "That's very kind of you, Mr. Robinson, but it wouldn't help, not in the long run. James Wentworth is my friend. I owe him a better answer than a lie."

"Why?" Squeaky said reasonably. "He did something for you that you got to pay back?"

"Not as simple as that," Henry answered. "But yes, I suppose so. Friendship. Being there over the years, knowing when to speak and when to keep silent. Sharing things because they mattered to me, even though not to him. Telling me about funny and interesting things he'd learned. Being open about his failures as well as his successes."

Squeaky had a glimpse of something new and perhaps beautiful. It was annoying, but he felt as if he had arrived somewhere just after the party was over. The music had stopped, but he could hear its echo.

Crow stood up. His face was masklike in the sallow light from the one lantern on the wall. "I'm pretty certain at least two people were killed here," he said quietly. "Very violently indeed. One here, where this blood is." He pointed to the largest stain on the ground. "Then it looks as if two people fought." He looked at splashes and smears, which were apparently trodden in several times by feet that seemed to have slipped and twisted on the edge of a larger stain. "And the other one was killed, or at least seriously injured, here. That effigy with the white lead face was right about that. Whether Lucien was one of the victims or not we need to find out."

"Yes," Henry agreed quietly. "Of course we do. And I suppose if he wasn't, we need to know what has happened to him, and . . . and if the victims were Sadie and Niccolo, then we need to know who killed them."

Squeaky was about to say that it could only have been Lucien, then changed his mind. Poor Henry had had enough for the moment. He must be exhausted, hungry, and cold, and none of them knew what time it was, or more than roughly even where they were.

Crow pushed his hands into his pockets. "We need to find someone else who knows Lucien and can tell us something of what happened here. To judge by how sticky the blood still is, it wasn't very long ago."

"What do you mean by 'not long ago'?" Squeaky said with a tremor in his voice. "An' where's the body anyway? That much blood, someone's dead, but how do we know if it was a man or a woman, let alone that it was Lucien?"

"We don't," Henry replied. "That's why we must find proof of this. Someone moved it. Where to, and why? And what is this place?"

"It's the passage between two clubs, of sorts," Squeaky answered, looking around them at the stained walls, some brick, some stone. "Or maybe more than two. I'll shake the bleedin' truth out of someone." He set off toward the light, then past it, and found a fork to the right. There was a whole network of tunnels under London that he knew about. Indeed, in the past he had used them himself. He had forgotten how dark they were, and he had intentionally forgotten the smell. It washed back on him now as if the years between had been erased and he was again a young man, hot-tempered, desperate, and greedy, buying and selling anything, especially people. It was more than distaste he felt, more than a clogging stench in his nose and throat.

Bessie was pulling on his coattails. He wanted to turn round and slap her away. She trusted him, and she had no right to. It was stupid, as if she were trying to remind him of all those other girls that he had put into the trade, faces he couldn't even remember now.

He stopped abruptly and she collided with him, hands still clinging on to the stuff of his coat.

"Stop it!" he snarled at her. "Don't follow me like . . ." He was going to say 'like a dog,' but that was too harsh, even if it was apt. She looked just like a loyal, trusting, stupid little dog that expected him to treat it right.

She let her hands fall, still looking at him,

which made him feel as if she had kicked him in the pit of his stomach.

"Like . . . like I could look after you," he finished. "Someone's got to find out what happened to the corpse. In't fit for you to see. Stay with Mr. Rathbone."

"I seen corpses," she told him, putting out her hand and taking hold of his coattails again. "I'll 'elp yer."

He blasphemed under his breath, and felt Henry Rathbone's eyes on him, even though he was farther from the light and his figure was only a shadow behind them.

"Aren't yer going on, then?" Bessie asked. "Yer in't given up, 'ave yer?"

Squeaky swore again, turning around to continue his way along the passage and up more steps to a door. Beyond it were sounds of music and laughter.

"No, I in't given up," he answered her at last. "But we've got to think what to do now. If Lucien's dead, that's the end of it."

"If it wasn't Lucien, then who was it?" Henry asked. "And even more important, who killed him, or her?"

"You mean, was it Lucien?" Crow said softly.

He looked at Henry. "Do you want to know that? What are we going to do if it was?"

Henry was silent for several moments. No one interrupted his thoughts.

"That may depend on the reasons," he answered at last, hope struggling in his voice, in what they could see of his face in the dim light. "Maybe it was self-defense. In a place like this that is imaginable."

Squeaky was torn between pity and the urgent desire to tell Henry not to be so naive. This was getting more ridiculous by the moment.

"Lucien wouldn't kill nobody less 'e 'ad ter," Bessie said at last. "If . . . if it weren't 'im as were killed."

"Right, Bessie," Henry agreed warmly. "We need to find anyone at all who has seen him in the last few hours—two or three, let us say. Please lead on, Mr. Robinson. If we can find Sadie, she may well know."

Squeaky bit back the words on the edge of his tongue, and started forward again.

They went from one tavern or doss-house to another all through the night and well into the cold, midwinter daylight. They shook people awake to ask about Lucien or Sadie. They threatened and promised. Squeaky lied inventively, while Henry persuaded—often with a few coins or a ham sandwich that he bought from a peddler—but no one would admit to knowing anything about murder. Even a hot cup of coffee from a stand on the corner of one of the alleys elicited nothing useful.

They found people huddled in doorways, covered with old clothes or discarded packing and newspapers, sometimes too drunk to even be aware of their freezing limbs. All questions about Lucien or Sadie were met with vacant stares. For most that was also true for any mention of Shadwell. The two or three who reacted did so with blank denial and with shivering more than was warranted by the cold of the icy morning.

They stopped at last for a hot breakfast at a tavern off Shaftesbury Avenue. There was a good fire in the hearth. Although the room was dirty and everything smelled of smoke and spilled ale, they sat at a scarred wooden table and ate bacon, eggs, and piles of hot toast, and drank fresh tea. Bessie managed to consume more than the other three together.

"What do we know?" Henry asked, looking at each of them in turn. "Somebody was killed at the bottom of those steps. There was too much blood for those wounds not to have been fatal." He turned questioningly to Crow.

"Yes," Crow agreed. "From the way it was placed, it could have been two people. Or it could have been one dead and one badly injured. It looked as if they had been dragged, but where to? Where are they now?"

"Why move them anyway?" Henry asked. "That's a question to which we need the answer. Buried decently, or just disposed of? Hidden to conceal who killed them, or who they were?"

"Or that they were killed at all," Crow added. "Except that they didn't wash away the blood. They could have done something about that."

"Rats'll get rid of that, in time," Squeaky pointed out.

Crow's face registered his distaste, but also a sudden spark of interest. "Then it can't have been there long," he observed. "No one we spoke to admitted to having seen anything at all." He leaned forward a little over the table. "Is that indifference, even to the bribe of food? Or are they too afraid to answer anyone? Is this man Shadwell's power so great?" He looked at Henry and Squeaky in turn. "Or is it that the murderer never came aboveground into the world in which we have been asking?"

Henry shivered, his face bleak with exhaustion, and the weight of the terrible new way of existence that had never entered his imagination before now. "I suppose there is nothing with which the police can help us?" he asked, but there was no hope in his eyes.

Squeaky nearly dropped his mug of tea, saving it with difficulty. "Damn." It would have ruined his bread and bacon. "Never!" He also narrowly avoided using the language that sprang to his mind. "We don't want the police in this," he said fervently. "If it's Lucien who's dead we don't want his father to find out this way. Then all the world'll know." He saw the alarm and the pity in Henry's face and how no more explanation was necessary.

"We have to know whether it was him or not," Henry said quietly. "How can we do that?" He looked first at Squeaky, then at Crow.

It was Bessie who answered, her mouth still full of toast.

"In't no use lookin' fer the corpses. If it's Shadwell wot done it, 'e'll put 'em where the rats'll get 'em. Rats are always 'ungry, an' bones all look the same."

Crow stopped eating, as if he could not swallow the bacon in his mouth.

Henry closed his eyes, then opened them again slowly. "Have you any idea where else we should look, Bessie?" he asked.

"'We can't find Sadie, we could look fer 'oo owned 'er,'" she replied. She took another piece of toast and bit into it, then wiped her hand across her chin to rub away the excess butter. "She's a fly piece, an' all, but worth summink. 'Ooever 'e is, 'e's goin' ter be as mad as 'ell if she's dead. Yer gotta look after yer property, or anybody'll take it from yer. 'E's gonna make sure as 'ooever did this pays fer it, so's it don't 'appen again. Keep respect, like."

She was suddenly conscious of the three men staring at her. She lowered her eyes and rubbed her sleeve across her chin, just in case there was still butter there. She wasn't used to food like this. In fact, she wasn't used to having her own food at all, specially set out for her alone, on a separate plate.

Squeaky knew she was right. He was annoyed that he hadn't thought of that himself. He should have! He really had to get out of Portpool Lane; his brain was curdling.

"Course," he agreed a little sourly. "That's the one thing we know. She were the woman dead, so someone's going ter be mad as hell, 'cause he's been robbed. By all accounts she were something real special. Drove men mad for 'er. Who knows how many more, before Lucien."

"Excellent," Henry approved wryly. "A little sleep, and then we shall begin again. That is, if you are all still willing? I would be extremely grateful for your help."

"Course," Bessie said immediately.

"Yer'd help anyone on two legs, fer a piece o' toast an' jam," Squeaky said with disgust.

She gave him a radiant smile. "'E don't 'ave ter 'ave two legs," she corrected him.

Henry and Crow both laughed aloud. Henry patted her gently on the shoulder. "I suggest we find somewhere with a place to sleep, reconvene at dusk for something to eat, and then continue on our way."

Crow turned to Bessie. "I'll find you somewhere." He stood up. "Come on."

She rose also and followed him obediently, leaving Squeaky feeling oddly alone. Crow was out of line: Squeaky was the one looking after her, not him. He did not notice Henry Rathbone's smile.

❖

*T*hey spent the greater part of the following night asking discreet questions of pimps, tavern-keepers, barmen, and other prostitutes. Again they bribed, flattered, and threatened. No one admitted to having seen Sadie, and it began to look more and more likely that she, and not Lucien, had been the victim. Unless there had been two corpses, and that was still unclear.

Some time toward morning the four of them sat in the corner of a public house in an alley off St. Martin's Lane, eating steak and kidney pudding with a thick suet crust and plenty of gravy. Outside the sleet was falling more heavily. Hailstones rattled on the window behind them. In the yellow circle of the lamplight on the pavement they could see the white drift of them filling the cracks between the cobbles.

"Cor! Sadie were a blinder, eh?" Bessie said with growing respect at what they had learned of her. "That Shadow Man must be ready ter tear the throat out o' 'ooever done 'er in." She shivered. "I'm glad I in't 'im. I reckon as 'e's goin' ter die 'orrible."

"I'm afraid you are right," Henry agreed. "But if it is she who was killed, it is hard to have much pity for him. If he were caught he would most certainly be hanged."

Bessie looked at Henry with a sudden gentleness. "It's a shame, 'cause Lucien were nice. I 'ope it weren't 'im. But if it were, 'e'll get worse, yer know. They always do."

"Yes, I imagine they do," he conceded softly.

Squeaky felt a sudden and overwhelming rage take hold of him. Damn Lucien Wentworth, and all the other idle, idiotic, self-absorbed young men who betrayed the love and privilege that was theirs and broke people's hearts by throwing away their lives. They had been given far more than most people in the world, and they had destroyed it, smeared filth over it until there was nothing left. It was a kind of blasphemy. He saw that for the first time, and it overwhelmed him. The whole idea of anything being holy had never occurred to him before.

"Do we agree that it is almost certainly Shadwell who owned her?" Crow asked, eating the very last of his pudding.

"Accounts conflict," Henry answered. "But at least some of the lies are clear enough to weed out. Shadwell seems to inspire a great deal of fear in people, which would suggest that he is the ultimate power in this particular world. Whoever is responsible for Sadie's death will be running from him, and he will be pursuing them." Without asking he refilled everyone's glass with fresh ale.

"But is it Lucien who killed her, or not?" Crow asked, directing his question at no one in particular.

"We will take Bessie's advice," Henry asserted. "We will look for whoever else is seeking the killer, because Shadwell will need to have vengeance for her death, even if only to preserve his own status. His resources will be immeasurably better than ours."

Squeaky sighed, his mind searching for an excuse to end this futile chase. Whatever they discovered, it wasn't going to be good. Either Lucien was dead, and in a way that his father would have nightmares about for the rest of his life, even if that wasn't long, or else Lucien had murdered the woman who had apparently betrayed him, if you could use that word for such a creature. Only an idiot, or a man drugged out of his wits, would have trusted her anyway. Squeaky had known many women of that sort. He had bought and sold them himself, not so very long ago. Well, none as beautiful as Sadie seemed to have been, but women anyway, some of them pretty enough. But he wasn't going to offer any advice on the subject because he would much rather Henry Rathbone didn't know that. Or Crow either, for that matter.

And if Lucien were still alive, then the situation was even worse. They'd have to lie. They could never tell his father about this. Better he think him dead.

"You know . . ." he began. Then he looked at Henry's face and realized he would be wasting his breath to argue.

❦

That evening they began to descend even deeper into the world of addiction and despair. The broad streets of the West End of London were glittering bright on the surface. They walked along Regent Street and into the Haymarket, passing theaters of the utmost sophistication. Bessie lagged behind, staring at the notices, the lights, the fashions. Several times Squeaky had to yank at her hand to drag her along.

The lamps were lit, and the gleam off of them caught the pale drifts of snow, touching it with warmth.

"Come on!" Squeaky said sharply, but Bessie was watching the carriages clattering up and down the center of the street, or swiveling around to look at people walking arm in arm, men with greatcoats on, women in capes trimmed with fur.

They turned off Piccadilly into an alley, and within twenty yards there were fewer lights, and in the shadowed doorways prostitutes plied their trade, ignoring those huddled within feet of them, half asleep, sheltering from the icy wind and the sleet.

Crow led the way down the steps from the pavement into a cellar, and through that into a deeper cellar. He began asking questions, discreetly at first, full of inventive lies.

"Looking for my sister," he explained, then described Sadie as well as he could, from other people's words.

A gaunt-eyed drunkard stared at him vacantly. "Don't know, old boy. Won't care," he drawled. "Got anything fit to drink?"

Crow passed by him, and Squeaky, still holding Bessie by the hand, spoke to a fat man with a face raddled and pockmarked with old disease.

"Lookin' fer a man who owes me money," he said grimly, then described Lucien. "I don't sell my women for nothing."

But the answer he received was equally useless.

They wasted little more time there before going out the back into a half-enclosed courtyard, then down more steps into a subterranean passage leading toward the river. Here there were more rooms indulging darker tastes. Even Bessie seemed disturbed. Squeaky could feel her fingers digging into his flesh, gripping him as if he were her lifeline.

Henry said nothing, perhaps too appalled to find words. They saw men and women, and those who might have been either, in obscene costumes, practicing torture and humiliation that belonged in nightmares.

Bessie shivered and leaned her head against Squeaky's shoulder.

Patiently Squeaky described Sadie and was greeted with raucous laughter from a man with hectic energy as if fueled by cocaine. His limbs twitched, and he seemed to find it difficult to contain his impatience.

"You too?" the man said, then laughed again.

"Someone else looking for her?" Squeaky said immediately.

"Yes! Oh yes! The long black hair, the beautiful eyes. Sadie—Sadie!"

"Who?" Squeaky urged.

Suddenly the man stood still, then he started to shiver.

"Who?" Squeaky lowered his voice. "Tell me, or I'll slit yer throat!"

Henry drew in his breath to protest, then changed his mind.

"Shadwell," the man replied very softly. Then he swiveled around, pushed his way between two men sharing a bottle, and disappeared.

Squeaky looked around at the vacant stares of the opium and laudanum addicts, the rambling half conversations of the drunkards, and gave up. He jerked his hand to direct them onward, and gripped Bessie more tightly as they followed a short, heavy man out into the alley.

Squeaky saw these people now with deepening disgust precisely because he had seen them all before. He had just forgotten the sheer and useless misery. Suddenly respectability, whether it dulled your wits or not, had a sweetness nothing else could match. It was like drinking clean water, breathing clean air.

Standing here in this filthy alley, he wanted to turn and run, escape before it caught hold of him again, or before he woke up and realized that everything he had now was just a dream. Hester Monk would despise him if she ever saw this. The thought of that made the sweat break out on his body in a way no physical fear ever had.

He hurried on, asking questions discreetly, in roundabout fashion, as if looking for pleasure himself.

It was obvious that Henry Rathbone found it repugnant to see people's misunderstanding as to his intent, but he offered no explanation. The distaste, the embarrassment lay in his eyes and the faint pulling of his mouth, almost impossible to read in the garish light of gaslamps. Squeaky saw it only because he knew it was there.

They did not mention Lucien's name, only his description, and regrettably there were many young men of excellent family and considerable means, even in the most depraved places, where any kind of sexual pleasure was for sale, the more bizarre the more expensive.

In one wide tunnel close to the river, laughter echoing along its length, magnified again and again, water dripping down the walls, Henry mentioned Shadwell again, as if it were half a joke. It was met with sudden silence. The blood drained from the skin of the man they were talking to, or perhaps it was a woman. In the flickering light and under the paint it was hard to tell. His naked shoulders were pearly white, blemishless, and without muscles, but his forearms were masked by long pink gloves, up to the elbow. Crow had seen such things before, but Henry was clearly uncomfortable. Still, he refused to let anything stop him in his quest.

"If you would be good enough," Henry persisted.

The man—or woman—froze. There was music playing somewhere, strident and off-key.

"You heard wrong," he said. His voice shook. "Someone's playin' you for a fool. I have to go." And with a surprisingly hard shove, he knocked Henry off balance so that Squeaky only just prevented him from falling.

Crow seized the man by the arm. "No names, just which way?" he demanded.

But it was no use. The fear of Shadwell was greater than anything Crow or Squeaky could call up.

They heard word of Lucien in several places, or at least of someone who might have been him. On the other hand, such a person might have been anyone, even Niccolo, Sadie's other lover.

"Why yer wanna know?" a short, monstrously fat man demanded, waddling around the bench in a brothel entrance to stare at them. His face was red, with a bulbous nose, crazed over its surface with broken veins. His flesh wobbled as he moved, and Bessie backed away from him, pushing herself hard against Squeaky's side.

The fat man looked her up and down, his eyes almost level with her throat. He lowered his gaze to her chest. "What d'yer want for 'er? There's some as like skinny bints, like they was children."

"She's not for sale," Henry snapped. "Touch her, and Mr. Robinson will break your fingers." He said it with perfect seriousness.

Squeaky drew in his breath to protest vigorously, then realized that perhaps if the man did touch Bessie, he would indeed be delighted to do something like that, or something even more personal.

The fat man stepped back, his eyes hot, his large hands clenched. Then, moving with surprising speed, he darted behind his bench again. His other hand plunged into the space between it and the wall, and came out brandishing the long, thin blade of a sword. The light glittered on its polished steel. It made a whiplike sound as he sliced it through the air.

Henry had nowhere to retreat; he was already against the wall. The little color in his face drained away as he realized his situation. Crow moved away, to distract the fat man's attention, but it was Squeaky who seized the hat stand by the door. Swinging it round like a long staff, he cracked it over the fat man's head, who crashed down, blood pouring from his scalp.

Henry stared at the widening pool in horror.

Squeaky dropped the stand and grabbed Henry by the arm, leaving Bessie to follow. "Come on!" he ordered. "Out of here!"

"But he's injured!" Henry protested. "Shouldn't we . . ."

Squeaky swore at him. Ignoring his protest, he half-pulled him off his feet, dragging him to the door and out into the alleyway. It was pitch-dark and he had no idea where they were going. It was important to simply get away from the brothel and the fat man bleeding on the floor.

They walked rapidly, crowding each other in the dark, ice-slicked alley, tripping over debris, and hearing rats scuttle away. They kept moving until they had gone at least a quarter of a mile, then finally stopped in an empty doorway sheltered from the wind, and well out of the light of the solitary street lamp.

"Thank you," Henry said quietly. "I'm afraid I was taken by surprise. A foolish thing to have allowed. I apologize."

"It's nothing." Squeaky spoke casually, but a sudden warmth welled up inside him. He was ridiculously, stupidly pleased with Henry's gratitude. For a moment he felt like a knight in shining armor.

They continued their pursuit. The winter day and the bitter cold of night were almost indistinguishable in the cellars and passages between one smoky, raucous room and another.

After half a dozen abortive leads as to where Niccolo and Sadie might be, they came to a small abandoned theater. A score of people lay on the floor half asleep. Some gave at least the impression of being together, clinging to each other's body warmth. One man lay alone, huddled over in pain, his arms wrapped around himself defensively. His dark hair was matted, but still thick.

Crow picked his way across the floor and bent down beside him. Squeaky saw, from where he stood a dozen feet away, that the sleeping man's face was gaunt, but still handsome in the dark, sensitive way Niccolo had been described to them.

Crow shook his shoulder. "Niccolo?" he said sharply.

The man stirred.

"Niccolo?" Crow shook him harder and the man pulled away with a gasp of pain.

Bessie started forward from Squeaky's side. "It in't Niccolo, that's Lucien!" she said urgently. "'E's 'urt." She clambered over the bodies, some cursing her, and bent down beside Crow. "Yer gotta do summink," she demanded. "'Ere! Lucien! It's me, Bessie. We come to 'elp yer."

Lucien stirred and half sat up, grunting with the effort, holding his left arm to his side. "Who the hell are you?" His speech was slurred but it still held the remnants of his origins, the home and the privilege to which he had been born.

The eagerness died out of Bessie's face. "Don't yer remember me?"

Lucien groaned.

"Of course he does," Crow said with sudden anger. "He's just half asleep, and he's hurt."

"Yer gonna 'elp 'im," she urged Crow.

Without answering, Crow pulled the coat Lucien was wearing away from him and looked at the wound. His shirt was matted with blood on the right side of his chest.

Lucien winced and swore. "Leave me alone!" he said with a burst of real fury. "Get out."

Henry stepped over a couple of sleeping figures and went to Crow and Lucien. He reached down and took Lucien's arm. "Stand up," he ordered. "Before we can help you, we need to get somewhere clean, where we can see what we're doing."

"I don't want your bloody help!" Lucien snapped. "Who the hell are you anyway?"

"My name is Henry Rathbone. Stand up."

Something in the authority of his tone made Lucien obey, but sullenly.

Squeaky also stepped forward. He could see

other people beginning to stir. A lone figure in the farthest archway was standing upright, one arm bent a little as if holding something, perhaps a weapon.

"We got ter get out of here," he said tersely to Henry and Crow. "You bring him." He gestured toward Lucien. "Give him a clip around the ear if he makes a fuss." He snatched Bessie's hand and almost pulled her off her feet. "C'mon."

They could not go far. Lucien was weak, and they had no idea how deep his wound was or how long ago he had sustained it. It was bitterly cold outside, and a steady, hard sleet was turning back to a soaking rain. Here in the passages and alleys so narrow that the eaves met overhead, the pall of smoke in the air was made worse by the fog blowing up from the river, so even at midday the light was thin and pale.

"We need to find somewhere to look at this," Crow said grimly. "And something to eat," he added.

They searched for more than an hour, asking for a room, space, anything private. All the time Crow and Bessie supported Lucien, who was rapidly growing weaker, and stumbling every few yards.

At last they found a back room in a pub. After a good deal of hard bargaining, threats from Squeaky, and money from Henry, they were shown to one small, dirty room with candles and a wood-burning stove, for which fuel was extra. Squeaky went to buy food and to find the nearest well to fill a bucket of water. Bessie swept the floor after very neatly stealing a neighbor's broom. She returned it with a charming smile, saying she had found it in the alleyway.

Crow and Henry did what they could to help Lucien. Crow, who still had his Gladstone bag with him, took out a length of clean bandage and a small bottle of spirit.

"This is going to hurt," he told Lucien. "But it'll hurt a hell of a lot more if you get gangrene in it. That could kill you."

Lucien glared at him. "What the hell do you care? Who are you, anyway? Who are any of you?"

"I'm a doctor," Crow replied, measuring the spirit out into a small cup.

"I'm not drinking that," Lucien told him.

"You're not being offered it," Crow replied. "It's to clean your wound. It'll sting like fire." Without hesitating he jerked Lucien's protective arm away from the wound and placed an alcohol-soaked bandage on it.

Lucien screamed. His voice choked off as he gagged and gasped for breath.

Bessie stared at Crow. Her face was ashen, but she said nothing.

Henry felt sick. He could barely imagine the pain. He looked at the wreck of a man lying on a pile of rags on the floor, the messy knife wound in his side now exposed, and he remembered the youth he had known a dozen years ago.

Crow's dark face was tense, his concentration on the tools of his art: the scalpel, the forceps, the needle and thread. He was an extraordinary young man, not much more than Lucien's age. Henry realized that he had spent the last four or five days in Crow's company, and yet he knew almost nothing about him. He did not even know his full name, much less where he came from, who his family were, or even where he lived.

He watched now as Crow bent to clean and stitch the gash in Lucien's side. His hands were lean and strong: beautiful hands. And his face was unusual: too mercurial to be handsome, too many teeth—that enormous smile. He was also skilled.

Henry wondered why he had not qualified as a doctor, but it would be grossly insensitive to ask, inexcusably so. He maintained his silence, simply handing him the instruments as he was asked for them.

It took a little while, and when Crow was finally satisfied, Lucien lay back on the rags, exhausted. "Thank you," he said with a gasp.

"What happened?" Crow asked.

"Someone stuck me with a knife," Lucien replied. "What the hell does it look like?" He was still speaking between gritted teeth.

"It looks like you were caught in a fight," Crow told him. "What happened to the person who stabbed you?"

"Why?" There was a faint flicker of a smile. "You want to go bandage him too?"

Crow ignored the question. "Are you injured anywhere else? Is there anything more I can do?"

"No." Lucien hesitated. "Thank you."

Crow put his instruments away and closed his bag. "I rather thought the other person might be dead—was it a man or a woman? Or one of each? Which was how they managed to strike back at you."

Lucien stared at him, moving a little so he

faced him, his eyes wide, his face fallen slack with amazement.

Crow waited, looking expectantly for an answer.

Slowly Lucien lay back, relaxing against the rags with a wince as his muscles pulled against the bandage.

"I didn't kill anyone," he said wearily. "It was a stupid fight over cocaine. Some idiot thought I had his and he attacked me."

"And did you?" Crow raised his eyebrows.

"I don't even use the damn stuff! I like opium . . . now and then." His eyes looked somewhere far away. "I'm drunk on life, on laughter and passion, on dreams of the impossible, on Sadie, and something that seems like love, or at least seems like not being alone." His voice dropped. "How in hell would you know what I'm talking about." It was a dismissal, not a question.

"No idea," Crow replied, his sarcasm barely discernible. "The rich are the only ones who have any idea what loneliness is, or loss, or the sense of having failed. The rest of us are too busy with hunger, cold, and disease, and finding somewhere to sleep for the night—or at least to lie down."

Lucien stared at him, and Crow stared straight back. Very gradually something in Lucien changed.

"I'm sorry," he said gently. "That was stupid. I despise self-pity. Most of all in myself."

Crow gave him one of his dazzling smiles. "So do I," he agreed.

Squeaky returned with food and water. Bessie portioned it out and carefully fed Lucien his share before eating her own.

When they were finished Henry turned to Lucien. "I came at your father's request," he stated simply. "He wants me to ask you to come home, but before that is possible, we need to clear up the matter of the murder of Sadie, or Niccolo."

Outside the wind was rising, rattling the windows.

Lucien gave a harsh bark of laughter. "Clear it up! You mean explain it? Somehow make it all right?" His mouth twisted with contempt. "You're an idiot. Go back and tell my father you couldn't find me. It's true enough. You have no idea who I am now, or what happened to the Lucien Wentworth you thought you knew."

"I intend to find out," Henry replied.

Lucien turned away. "You wouldn't understand."

"Don't be so incredibly arrogant," Henry said

sharply. "Do you think you are the first young man to indulge himself and throw away the life he was given? To tell other people that they wouldn't understand is to give yourself a uniqueness you don't possess. You are desperately and squalidly ordinary. The only thing different about you is that you had more to throw away than most of us."

Now Lucien was angry. "And what the hell would you know about it? You comfortable, complacent, self-satisfied . . ." He trailed off.

"Self-pity again?" Henry inquired.

"Self-disgust," Lucien replied quietly. "Go back and tell my father that you couldn't find me. It's not a lie. You couldn't find the son he wants back. That man died a year ago."

"Who killed him? You? Or Sadie?"

Lucien gave an abrupt laugh. "Very good. I did. Sadie only helped."

"Where did you meet her?" Henry asked.

"At the theater, with friends. She came to the party afterward." He smiled briefly and for a moment he was lost in another time. "God, she was beautiful! She made every other woman in the room seem half-alive, leaden creatures without color, as if they lived in the shadows."

"Like Shadwell," Henry remarked.

Lucien's eyes widened. "Don't even whisper his name," he said very quietly. "There was nothing of that in Sadie then. She was just . . . so alive. It was as if she could see the magic in everything. And she liked me. You think that's my delusion, my vanity? It isn't. There were loads of other men there with titles, and more money than I'll ever have."

Henry said nothing.

"She liked me," Lucien repeated, but his voice wavered a little this time, the certainty gone.

"Of course," Henry agreed. "And it is very pleasant to be liked."

For an instant there was a devastating loneliness in Lucien's face, then anger. "She didn't ask for anything," he said sharply. "Never money. She was more fun than any other woman I've known. She knew how to dress, how to dance, how to be funny and wise and more original than anyone else. She made the rest of them look like cows! Half asleep most of the time. Never saying anything except placid agreement, whatever they think you want them to say. I wouldn't be surprised to see most of them chewing the cud!"

"And she found you equally interesting," Henry

observed, a slightly dry amusement in his voice. "That must have been most agreeable for you."

"It was," Lucien snapped. Then suddenly he seemed to crumple, and sweat broke out on his forehead.

Crow looked across at Henry, frowning a little.

"Where is Sadie now?" Henry asked. "Is she the one who was murdered, or was it Niccolo?"

"I don't know. I think it was Niccolo," Lucien replied.

"If you don't know, that means you haven't seen either of them."

"Yes," Lucien agreed hoarsely. "I don't know!"

Henry allowed his gaze to wander around the cold room again, with its dark walls, its filthy windows now rattling in the wind.

"Your father would welcome you home," he said, looking at Lucien again.

The color burned up Lucien's face. "I can't come," he said very quietly, avoiding Henry's eyes.

"Why not?" Henry asked.

"Shadwell—Shadow Man," Lucien replied. "I . . . I do things for him. I owe him."

There was silence for a few minutes. Squeaky put another piece of wood in the stove. They'd be lucky if it lasted the night. Outside the rain was running down the gutters and dropping from the eaves. Bessie sat next to Squeaky, close to him for warmth.

"Did you kill Sadie?" Henry asked Lucien.

Lucien's eyes opened wide. "No!"

"Or Niccolo?"

"No! I can't think of any reason you should believe me, but I haven't killed anyone, at least . . . at least not directly. God knows what I've caused indirectly. Poor Sadie. It was a hell of a mess." His face pinched with remembered pain, and his eyes seemed to see the memory as if it were more real than Henry himself, or Crow sitting on the floor a few feet away.

"But you saw it?" Henry challenged.

"Only the blood," Lucien replied.

"What is it you do for Shadwell?" Henry asked.

"Bring people here—young ones with money."

Lucien started to shudder. His body seemed to slip out of his control, and his teeth rattled.

Henry took off his coat and wrapped it around Lucien, folding it over his thin body with gentleness. Then he sat back on the ground again, looking oddly vulnerable in his shirtsleeves.

Bessie looked at him anxiously, but Squeaky put out his hand to stop her from interrupting.

If Henry was cold, he gave no sign of it.

"Bring people here to indulge their tastes, and then they find that they are addicted, and have to come back again and again? And if they become troublesome, who deals with them then?"

"I don't know," Lucien stammered through his teeth. "Shadwell himself, maybe."

"Was Sadie troublesome? Was she no longer doing what he wanted of her?" Henry persisted.

Lucien stared at him. Then he closed his eyes and turned away. "She always did what he wanted. She couldn't afford not to."

"Why not?"

"Don't be so damn stupid!" Lucien gave an abrupt, painful laugh that ended in choking. When he caught his breath again he went on. "He gave her the pretty things she liked, and the cocaine she needed."

"So then why did he kill her?"

"I don't know. Maybe it wasn't him."

"Niccolo?"

"I don't know. He could be dead too." Lucien gulped. "Maybe it was that verminous little toad in the lavender velvet."

"Ash. Why would he kill them?"

"I don't know."

Henry waited.

Lucien sighed. He looked away, avoiding Henry's eyes. "I've crossed a few people, made enemies. If Niccolo is dead, whoever killed him probably thought it was me. We looked rather alike. In the half light of that passage, and if he was with Sadie . . ." He stopped. His face filled with regret and a peculiar kind of pain that was extraordinarily honest, without self-pity, as if he could see his loss with new clarity. "We were always headed to destruction, she and I."

Crow looked at Henry, his expression anxious.

Henry nodded and moved away, allowing Lucien to rest, at least for a while.

*B*essie was looking after Lucien, who was lying close to the stove. Henry Rathbone sat in the corner with Squeaky and Crow, who were huddled in their coats. They were saving the last few pieces of wood for the early morning.

"What do we look for now?" Henry asked, a note of desperation in his voice.

"Pick him up an' carry him out," Squeaky said

impatiently. "Before he gets us killed. Let his father deal with it."

Crow gave him a black look. "And of course this Shadwell will just let that happen! Next thing they know, the police will come to Wentworth's door looking for Lucien for the murder of whoever it was who was knifed to death at the bottom of those stairs."

Henry straightened up. "Then we need to know who it was, and who killed them."

"And if it was Lucien?" Crow asked him.

Henry bit his lip. "Then we find out how . . . and why, and decide what to do about it." He was sitting with his back against the wall, the candlelight accentuating his features. Rathbone looked appallingly tired, and yet there was no anger in his face, no bitterness that Squeaky could see. Of course he was a fool. Without Squeaky and Crow to look after him he would have come to grief in minutes. He would have been robbed blind, possibly killed if he had put up any resistance. He seemed to believe anything he was told, no matter how obviously a lie.

And yet there was a kind of courage in him that Squeaky had to grudgingly admire. And in spite of the stupid situation Henry had gotten them all into, Squeaky also rather liked him. That was another thing that had gone badly wrong lately: Since Squeaky had become respectable he had gone soft. Was this age catching up with him? Or cowardice? He had always been careful, all his life; to do otherwise would have been stupid. But he was never a coward! All his values had slithered around into the wrong place! Everything was out of control!

"Makes sense," Squeaky said at last. "If it's Sadie who's died, can't see why he would kill her. Seems to have been fascinated with her. She's the reason he got into this cesspit anyway. Likes his pleasures, that one. See it in his face when he talks about her. You get dependent on something, the bottle or the opium or whatever, then you don't destroy it. Those things make you act like an idiot, but they get to be the most important things in the world to you. You never, ever forget to keep them safe. You'd poke your mother's eyes out before you'd risk losing them."

"What if Sadie preferred Niccolo, and Lucien killed her in jealousy?" Henry asked.

"He'd kill Niccolo," Squeaky answered. "Taking her back. That's property. You don't smash something that's yours. It would just be stupid. Slap her around a bit, maybe," he conceded, remembering a few such acts of discipline from his brothel days. "Not where it shows, of course. Don't spoil the goods. So if it's him who's dead, we're in trouble."

Henry's face twisted with bitter amusement and understanding.

Squeaky blushed. He had not meant to give himself away so clearly. He would rather Henry merely guessed at his former life, rather than know it for certain. He wondered whether to try to improve on what he had said, then knew he would only make it worse.

"Do you think he is telling the truth?" Henry pressed. "And he really doesn't know who's died?"

"Not sure I'd go that far!" Squeaky protested. "Not . . . not entirely. He's bound to lie about some things."

Henry smiled.

Squeaky realized that he had just given himself away again. Now Henry would know that Squeaky always lied, at least a bit. Damn! Being respectable was a pain, and hard work!

Henry turned to Crow. "And you?"

"I've no need to lie," Crow said with a grin,

glancing at Squeaky, then away again. He straightened his face, suddenly very sober. "And I don't
think Lucien has either. He's pretty well lost,
whatever he says. No point really. Whether he did
kill either one of them or not, he's going to get
blamed for it. Personally I think it was probably
that disgusting little vampire in the lavender
coat. He looks like something risen from the dead.
I should think he likes knives."

"I believe him too," Henry said quietly.

"Hey, just a minute!" Squeaky protested. "I
didn't say I believed him. I just . . ." His mind
raced. "What if Sadie told Niccolo to go to hell, and
he killed her? Then Lucien comes along, sees her
dead an' covered in blood, an' he slices him up?
Ash had nothing to do with it."

Henry thought about it for several moments.
"Then why would Lucien not admit that?" he
asked. "Such an act would be justified, to the people here. And it seems they are all he cares about.
This is his world—at least until we can get him
out of it."

"Out of it?" Squeaky said incredulously. "Look
at him! He's drunk an' he's taking God knows
what else to keep him awake, or asleep, make him
laugh, or see what he wants to see, feel something

like being alive, God help him. He belongs here. Hell don't let go of people, Mr. Rathbone. Not that most people are willing to climb out of it, even if they could—an' they can't."

"First we have to find out if he killed either of the two victims, and if he did not, then who did."

"You asked us if we believe him that he didn't kill either of them," Crow interrupted. "And you say you do."

"I do," Henry agreed. "It is not a certainty, of course, but I shall treat it as such, unless circumstances should make that impossible. Therefore we must proceed on the assumption that someone else killed whoever it was—even both of them." He looked at Crow again. "What is your opinion of Mr. Ash?"

"Syphilitic," Crow said simply.

Henry was surprised. "You know that so easily?"

Crow smiled, but there was no pleasure in his expression. "He moved very little, but his hand slipped on the cane, as if he were not sure whether he gripped it or not, as if he could not really feel his fingers. His feet were the same. That curious, slightly stamping gait is peculiar to advanced stages of damage to the nerves. He is probably more than a little insane."

"Then he might well have been violent," Henry concluded.

"Why would he kill them?" Squeaky asked. "Even a creature like that has to have a reason."

"You are quite right," Henry agreed. "But one thing makes me wonder about the cane. Ash is quite small, and you say he has the signs of advanced syphilis?" He looked at Crow. "The cane in his hand slipped from his grasp. We saw it. Do you believe he could have attacked a healthy young man or woman and escaped completely unhurt himself?"

"Not likely," Crow conceded.

"Lucien," Squeaky said sadly. "He killed Niccolo, his rival for the girl, probably taking him by surprise—knife in the back. Then when she found them he attacked her too. That's where he got injured himself." He looked at Henry's downcast face and felt guilty for having spoken the truth when he knew it would hurt him. "You can't do anything for him."

Crow pulled his coat tightly around his shoulders. He had been staring at the ground, but now he turned to Henry. "We should put together all the evidence we can," he said, looking from Henry to Squeaky and back again. "Even here,

112

there has to be reason in things. There are a lot of questions we haven't answered yet. What do we know about this Niccolo? Who was he and where did he come from? Did he and Lucien know each other before meeting here? In fact, did Lucien bring Niccolo here? Or the other way round?" He stopped for a moment, looking from one to the other.

"Was it for women, or opium?" he went on. "Some kind of torture, or sexual appetite? Was Niccolo a sadist? A masochist? Did he love Sadie, or was he just using her?"

Henry smiled at him. "Thank you, Dr. Crow," he said gravely. "You are a voice of hope where there seems to be very little otherwise. Your suggestions are excellent. As soon as we have had a little sleep—if such a thing is possible in this place—we shall find something fit to eat, for ourselves and Lucien and Bessie, then continue our investigation." He looked at Crow, then at Squeaky, his face grave. "If you are still agreeable to helping, of course?"

Crow shrugged. "I'm curious," he said. "I'll help."

Henry waited for Squeaky.

Squeaky felt trapped. He should have resented

it, yet against all reason or sense, he was vaguely flattered to be included. He certainly would have been hurt had Henry not asked him. But he had to put up some sort of resistance, even if only to salvage the shreds of his reputation.

"Won't do any good," he said yet again. He gestured toward where Lucien was lying curled over on his unwounded side, either asleep or unconscious. "What else are you going to do with him anyway? If he killed Sadie and Niccolo, are you going to expect his father to take him in and cover it up? They may have been rubbish, but they were still people. And who'll he kill next, eh? Have you thought of that?"

"Yes, Mr. Robinson, I have," Henry said in little more than a whisper. "Nobody comes out of a place like this without paying a price, and I am not imagining that Lucien can do so either. I want to help him, not to excuse him. It is not a physical thing, to climb out of hell, as you put it; it is an ascent of the spirit. It will be long and extremely painful, and there is a cost to be paid. It is a steep climb—a toll road if you like—and each stretch of it will exact a price. But I imagine you know that."

Squeaky was stunned. He stared at Henry's

ashen face with its clear blue eyes, and saw no evasion in it, no soft, easy forgiveness. Was Henry referring to Squeaky's own ascent from a place not as unlike this as he would wish to imagine it, until he was now positively decent? Or very nearly. Hester Monk treated him as if he were honest. Of course she probably kept a very good check on him, although he had never caught her doing so. That was a painful thought too. He very much liked having her trust. It was worth quite a lot of discomfort to keep it.

Henry was still watching him.

It occurred to Squeaky that in helping Lucien Wentworth, he might be proving that the way up was possible, proving it to Henry Rathbone, and more than that, to himself.

"Course I'll help," he said tartly. "You need me. I know a lot of things you don't."

Henry smiled, extraordinarily sweetly. "For which I am grateful," he accepted. "Now let us rest until it is time to begin."

They slept briefly, then set out to find some hot food, and perhaps pies and ale they could bring back for Lucien and Bessie. They left the alleys and walked along Piccadilly into Regent Street. It was dry now and bitingly cold, with frost and here and there a dusting of snow, which contributed to the decorations of colored ribbons and wreaths of holly and ivy on shop doors.

"Happy Christmas!" a stout woman called out cheerfully, passing sweets to a child.

"And to you!" a gentleman returned. "Happy New Year to you!"

Someone was singing "God rest ye merry gentlemen" and other voices joined in.

The traffic was heavy, the clatter of hooves and the jingle of harnesses loud.

Squeaky rolled his eyes, and said nothing.

"Happy Christmas," Henry replied to a passerby.

After another hundred yards they found a tavern serving hot food that had a good fire in the hearth. Henry paid for them all, including provisions to take back to Bessie and Lucien. They ate in silence, relishing the luxury too much to disturb the pleasure of it with conversation.

They started back again and were soon in the narrow alleys. It was dim, as if it were always dusk on these midwinter days. There was no reality of Christmas here, perhaps not even any belief in its meaning.

They delivered the pies and ale, which were received with gratitude, expressed with few words and ravenous pleasure. They decided that Bessie would stay with Lucien to look after him while he healed. Henry, Crow, and Squeaky would continue to search for proof of who had been killed, and whether Lucien was involved or not, and if so, in what way.

It was decided that Crow would go back to Mr. Ash and see if he could persuade him to tell whatever else he knew.

"There has to be more," Henry said. "He is involved in it somehow, because he feels too intensely to simply be an observer."

Crow agreed. "What about you?" he asked.

Henry bit his lip. "I shall endeavor to learn something of this Niccolo—who he is, and above all if anyone has seen him in the last two days." He looked at Squeaky. "You are the best suited among us to learn more about Sadie, particularly if she is still alive, and if not, who else, apart from Lucien, would have wanted to kill her."

Squeaky considered that a very dubious compliment, but this was not the time to argue with what was clearly the truth. Henry himself would be totally useless at such a task.

They agreed to meet back at daybreak the following morning, at the latest.

The others were already waiting when Squeaky returned, carrying a jug of hot chocolate he had purchased with some money he had "liberated" from a less-deserving owner. He shared it, measuring carefully, then sat down on the floor to enjoy his portion.

Henry turned to Crow, his eyebrows raised questioningly.

Crow warmed his hands on his mug.

Henry had bought some pies. Squeaky refrained from asking what was in them; he preferred to imagine. He also did not ask what they had cost. Both were things he very much preferred not knowing.

The candles were getting low. One had already guttered and gone out. Lucien and Bessie were probably asleep. They had already checked on them, Crow with some concern.

"How ill is Ash?" Henry asked. "Could he have killed them?" His face was in shadow, so Squeaky could not read his expression, but he heard the strain in his voice. Rathbone must have seen things here that his quiet life on Primrose Hill had not prepared him even to imagine. And of course there was always the smell. Few middle-class people had experienced the smells of the gutter, the sewage, the decaying bodies of rats, the rot of old wood.

It brought back memories to Squeaky that he had worked very hard to forget.

Before the security of Portpool Lane there had been other places, ones that smelled like this, of stale wine, vomit, unwashed bodies, blood, and sweat. Above all he could remember the fear. It might be the sudden eruption of temper into a blow against the head, or the knife in the stomach of deliberate revenge. He never looked at his own body because he did not want to see the scars. Some had been from women, and that was better forgotten too. Perhaps he had deserved those, or at least some of them.

Hate was behind him now. Some people even trusted him, and that was like a delicate, precious flame in the darkness. He would kill to keep that, and the moment he did, of course, it would be gone, probably forever. Damn caring what people thought. It was against all the laws of survival. And yet it still beguiled him and drew him in.

It seemed that Crow was going to answer Henry's question about Ash. He was sitting with his back against the wall, his enormously long legs straight out in front of him. There was a hole in the sole of his left boot. His face was more deeply lined than Squeaky had ever seen it before. He looked more like forty-five than thirty-five. Squeaky recognized it as not just weariness but a kind of pain that darkened the energy of spirit and the hope that lit him. If that went out, it would be a darkness Squeaky would never find his way out of.

Henry was watching him, waiting.

"He isn't going to live much longer," Crow said quietly. "His body's rotting. He stands so still because he can't feel his hands or feet. If he moves he's likely to lose his balance. He pretends to carry the stick for an affectation, but actually he'd fall without it. I don't think he killed Niccolo or Sadie, but he knows who did. In fact, I think he was there. He knows something else, but I can't get him to tell me."

"At a price," Squeaky told him. "Don't give all your help away. I know you're a doctor, an' all that, but doctors charge."

An indescribable expression crossed Crow's face. For a moment Squeaky was afraid he would not be able to pretend that he had not seen it. He realized with a jolt that in spite of the years he had seen him coming and going, watched him patch up the injuries of all manner of people, he really knew Crow very little: not the man underneath the black coat, the flashing smile, and the bizarre humor. Now he had trespassed, to a place Crow did not want to let him into.

"I have nothing to give him," Crow said, without looking at either Squeaky or Henry. "His pain is beyond anyone's reach. He is closed in with it until it kills him."

Squeaky shuddered. Perhaps in a way that was true of all of them, a final aloneness. He disgusted himself by feeling sorry for the man in his absurd costume.

Henry leaned forward. "Is it who killed them that he will not tell you?" he asked Crow. "Or something else?"

Crow thought for a moment. "I think it is something else," he said finally.

"The reason they were killed?" Henry suggested.

Squeaky stared at Crow, then at Henry, then back at Crow again.

"It's something about Sadie," Crow answered. "Something secret, that he nurses inside him, because he knows and we don't. We are making a profound mistake about her. Something we believe is totally wrong. I'm trying to work out what it could be, and I can't."

"Do you think Lucien killed her?" Henry asked. Squeaky knew from the tightness in his voice that if Crow said "yes," he would accept it.

Crow looked at Henry as if Squeaky were not even there.

"No," he answered. "Because he had no reason to. She gave him the physical pleasure that he craves, and she was very skilled, by all accounts, at making men feel admired, important—even that she loved them, in her own way. I can't see how he would have deliberately sacrificed that."

"That's more or less what I learned too," Henry agreed. "Pleasure, admiration, a kind of emotional power are his weaknesses, but not violence. It seems the same was true of Niccolo, from what I could find out."

"Jealousy?" Squeaky put in. "Most men get violent if the women they think of as theirs pay too much attention to someone else. I've seen it over and over. You don't have to be in love. It's to do with possession, with being top. If someone can take your woman away from you, it's a sign that you're weak. You could love anybody at all, so your love is meaningless." He forced memories away from him, things he had done in the past to make sure no one imagined him vulnerable, the fear he had instilled to keep himself safe. He could still too easily see their pale faces in his mind.

Henry and Crow were both looking at him.

Squeaky felt as if the ugliness in his mind were visible in his face, and they could read it. They would be revolted. He was revolted himself. He felt naked in the most painful and degraded way. His skin must be burning.

"They said she was beautiful," he began defensively. "Beauty can have funny effects on men. Lucien said it himself. Long black hair like silk, and sea-blue eyes. Sort of mouth you never forget. Comes into your dreams, whether you want it to or not."

"If that is the sort of woman she was, she may have had other enemies," Henry pointed out. "I know you are playing devil's advocate, Squeaky, which we need, but you must grant that that is also true."

"I know the devil too well to make jokes about him," Squeaky said grimly. "Or to plead anything for him either."

"I mean that you are making the opposite argument, so that we see our case in the full light, from all sides," Henry explained. "I was asking about Niccolo, but I learned a lot more about Sadie from the answers. She was very beautiful, and funny at times—although people who are drunk, or in love, are more easily amused than the rest of us."

He shook his head. "Even so, she seems to have been extraordinarily vivid in her personality, never a bore, which to some is the ultimate sin. But she was dependent on the cocaine, and without it she was very frightened." He stopped, his face in the shadow. "I think she may have had an illness, perhaps something like tuberculosis. What do you think, Crow?"

"I think you're probably right," Crow said softly. "Some of her vitality, some of her wild gulping at life was fear. I've seen it before. Do everything now, in case there's no tomorrow." He stopped abruptly.

Henry looked at him, then touched him very gently on the arm for just a moment before letting his hand fall.

Crow took a deep breath and let it out in a sigh.

"Is that right?" Squeaky asked. "Would she have died anyway? And you reckon she knew that?"

"I don't know whether she knew it," Crow replied.

"You're a doctor—you know!" Squeaky accused.

"I'm not a doctor." Crow looked at the ground.

Squeaky drew in his breath to ask him why not, then knew it would be intrusive, even cruel. You did not ask people questions like that. Crow was his friend, and friends do not trespass into pain, still less into failure.

"But it sounds like it," Crow went on. "The fever, bright eyes, pale skin with a flush on the cheeks, the frantic energy and the tiredness, the . . . the knowledge inside her that she has not long—the need to do everything now."

"You sound very sure," Henry said gently.

"I've seen lots of it," Crow replied, his voice cracking. He took a breath as if about to say something further, then let it out again without speaking.

Squeaky looked at Henry.

"No one can help that." Henry turned to Crow.

Crow smiled, his eyes filled with pain. "I used to think I could, when I was young, and stupid. My mother had it. That's why I wanted to be a doctor. I used to think I could cure her. But she died anyway."

"We all fail at something," Henry told him very quickly. "One way or another. Things that don't work out as we had hoped, people we love who don't love us, dreams that crumble. Time catches up with us, and we realize what we haven't done, what chances for kindness, for courage we have wasted, and too many of them won't come again. We see glimpses of what we could have been, and weren't."

Squeaky was stunned. What was this life Henry was talking about? It was surely not the life he had had himself, inventing and making things, having a son who was the best lawyer in London, a nice house, people who trusted and admired him. What failure had he ever known?

Henry's attention was on Crow. "But you have helped many," he said with growing conviction in his voice. "More important, you have helped some whom possibly no one else would help. Don't let yourself be crippled because it wasn't everyone. Nobody succeeds all the time." He smiled bleakly. "Think how insufferably arrogant we would become if we did. There would be no need for God."

Squeaky smiled. "Is He going to pick up the bits we drop, then?"

"I don't know," Henry replied. "But I don't mean to drop Lucien if I can help it. There's always a chance."

"You're a dreamer," Squeaky told him. "This isn't your world."

"Hell is everybody's world, at one time or another, Squeaky," Henry answered.

Squeaky blasphemed softly under his breath. "You've been here for days and you still don't have the least idea! Lucien's here because he wants to be!" He forced the words out between his teeth. He did not want to hurt this gentle man. He liked him, dammit! But somebody had to save him from himself.

Crow was staring at Squeaky.

"And you don't need to look like that either!" Squeaky snapped at him. "He came here for pleasure, no matter what it cost, or who paid it. He wanted to live in a world where everybody flattered him and told him how handsome and clever he was. He wanted to believe the lies—so he did. He didn't give a damn about anyone else, and now nobody gives a damn about him." He looked at Henry. "He's here because he chose it. And you can't change that."

"Of course I can't," Henry admitted. "But if he chooses to leave, perhaps I can help him believe that he can do it."

"It's too late," Squeaky said brutally, not because he wished to hurt, but because he couldn't bear the hope and despair that would follow. It had to end now.

"It's never too late," Henry said stubbornly. "Well, maybe it is sometimes, but not yet. There's still something to fight for. You are free to go, of course, but I would rather you stayed with us, because we need your help, and your experience."

Squeaky wanted to swear, but no words in all his wide vocabulary were adequate to suit his feelings.

"Well, I've got to stay, haven't I!" he said roughly. "You haven't got enough sense to find your way out of a wet paper bag!"

"Thank you," Henry said gravely.

"I've been thinking." Crow measured his words. "I've heard a lot about Sadie, because I asked about her. At least some of it has to be lies, but I can't tell which is which. Sorting out the truth might be our next course of action." He looked hopefully at Henry, then at Squeaky.

"So what did you hear?" Squeaky asked. "She's

a damn good whore, with T.B., and any other disease she might have picked up along the way. She had long, black hair and blue eyes."

"She was tall and slender, with extraordinary grace," Crow added. "And very disturbing eyes, actually, according to those who were not in love with her. One was green and one hazel."

Squeaky shrugged. "What does it matter?"

"Unless it was two different women?" Henry pointed out. "Maybe it wasn't even Sadie at all? Then Lucien would have had no reason to kill Niccolo." A sudden hope lit his face.

"Lucien is vain, stupid, completely selfish, and up to his eyeballs on opium, drink, and anything else he can get hold of!" Squeaky said. "He doesn't need a reason to lose his temper and kill someone!"

"But there was another woman Niccolo used," Crow argued. "Perhaps she was the one with the hazel-green eyes?"

"Can we find her?" Henry asked eagerly. "Do you know her name? Anything about her?"

"Rosa," Crow said, yawning. "Apparently he hit her quite a bit. I asked if we could find her, but no one's seen her recently."

"What does she look like?" Henry asked. "She

must be somewhere. Perhaps she's hiding because she knows what happened. Maybe she has a pimp who protects her . . . and he killed Niccolo, and Sadie just got in the way." He looked at Squeaky. "Or maybe it has nothing to do with Sadie. What do you think?"

Squeaky saw the hope in his eyes and hated to crush it. "Maybe," he said reluctantly. "I suppose. But if nobody's seen this woman, I don't know how we're going to find her."

"Look for her protector?" Henry suggested.

"Pimp, that's what you mean. The man who owns her."

Henry winced. "If you prefer."

"What if her pimp is Shadwell himself?" Squeaky asked, shifting his position because his legs were cramped. Hell, it was cold down here! He longed for the warmth of the Portpool Lane Clinic. "Do we want to go after him?" he added.

"He's the one with the opium, and probably the cocaine," Henry pointed out.

Then Squeaky had a sudden, wild idea, one that would really give them something to follow, if it were true. He leaned forward eagerly. "At first we didn't know if it was Lucien or Niccolo who was murdered," he said urgently. "We got different descriptions of Sadie, so maybe we don't know if it was Sadie who was killed, or this Rosa! Maybe nobody's seen her for a few days because she's dead!"

Crow stared at him, his eyes wide. "Nobody's seen Sadie either!" he argued, but he was leaning forward, wide awake now.

"We don't know that, 'cause we haven't been looking for Sadie," Squeaky pointed out.

"But why would anyone kill Rosa?" Henry asked, clearly puzzled.

"Well, maybe we should ask Lucien that." Squeaky replied. "Maybe there's a whole lot we should ask him, like exactly what he's done for Shadwell lately. Who else has he brought down here? Maybe there's someone in this we don't even know about." Squeaky drew in his breath and began again. "And let's ask Lucien what he knows about this Shadwell, an' make damn sure we get a straight answer this time. If Shadwell is Rosa's pimp, is he Sadie's too? And if he is, what does Lucien pay for her, and what else does he do to earn it?"

"You are right." Henry spoke before anyone else could. "We shall speak with Lucien again. However, I would be grateful if you would allow me to lead the questions." He pulled himself to his feet, a little stiffly. He had been sitting on the hard floor for some time like the others. He was cold, and his muscles locked when he tried to pull his coat more closely around him. It flapped open now as he walked across to where Lucien was huddled, half asleep.

Bessie looked up from where she sat with him, her face streaked with dirt, her eyes hollow. "I think 'e's a bit better," she said hopefully.

Henry knelt down. "Good. Thank you. I'm afraid we must disturb him because we have questions."

She nodded.

"Lucien," Henry said firmly. "Sit up and pay attention. I need to talk to you, as do Crow and Squeaky. There are many questions that cannot wait any longer."

Lucien stirred and opened his eyes. His face was almost colorless and shadowed with bruises. His cheeks were gaunt, but even so he did not seem quite as deeply shocked as he had a day earlier.

Henry moved to assist him in sitting up, and Bessie quickly helped him from the other side. He moved awkwardly and was queasy with pain, for a moment gagging as the wound in his side was stretched and the dried blood tore at his skin. At last he was propped against the wall.

"I don't know who killed him—or her," he said, biting his lips with pain.

"I assumed not." Henry said, moving to sit more comfortably. Crow and Squeaky were close, just a little behind him. "There are other things that matter, and may lead us to knowing who did."

"Nothing matters, Mr. Rathbone," Lucien contradicted him. "And it really won't make any difference. Either Sadie or Niccolo is dead, and everyone will believe I killed them, whoever really did."

"Shut up and answer what you're asked!" Squeaky told him curtly. "Mr. Rathbone decides what matters, not you."

Lucien gave a faint smile, looking at Henry. "Who's your charming friend?"

"Squeaky Robinson," Henry replied. "And for the moment he's right. There are several things we don't know, and it's necessary that we learn."

Lucien looked away.

Squeaky wondered if he was crafting some sort of lie that might excuse him. Or perhaps the man was simply afraid. For an instant Squeaky felt a surge of pity. It startled him. He knew better than that. Spoiled, arrogant young men like Lucien Wentworth had had everything given to them, all the privileges Squeaky himself had never even dreamed of! A safe home that was warm even in winter, enough food, even good food, clean and well-cooked, not anyone else's leftovers. They had beautiful clothes, always clean. People cared about what happened to them. They were taught to read, write, count, and speak like gentlemen. They didn't have to worry and be afraid of tomorrow.

So why was Squeaky sorry for him? Was it just because Hester would have been? Or was this all because of Henry Rathbone?

"Lucien," Henry said firmly. "I can't protect you, and I wouldn't even if I could. The only way out of this is to face it. And believe me, there is no escape. The pain is going to come, and the darkness, whether you run away or not."

Squeaky winced. He had wanted to interrupt; now he changed his mind. Henry's quiet voice was worse than anger or open emotion.

Lucien looked back at Henry. "I don't know who was killed, or who did it," he said again. "If Shadwell comes to take me himself, I still won't know. There's no use in you threatening; I can't help."

"I believe that is what you think," Henry replied. "Tell me more about Shadwell. Is he Rosa's pimp? And Sadie's?"

"He's Sadie's," Lucien answered. "At least . . . he owns her."

"And Rosa's pimp?" Henry asked.

"No." Lucien sounded doubtful, but he did not add anything more.

"Why Sadie's?" Henry persisted.

"Because he feeds her the cocaine she needs," Lucien replied quietly.

"And Rosa?"

"She didn't use it."

"Why does he feed Sadie cocaine?" Henry persisted.

Lucien did not reply but Squeaky could see him chewing his lip, biting. It must have hurt, but clearly less than the pain that burned inside him.

"She lures the kind of men few other women can," he replied reluctantly. "And she keeps them. They come again and again." A wry self-mockery lit his eyes and then went out.

Henry put his hand on Lucien's wrist, gripping him gently, but without allowing escape. "And why does he want you? What do you do for him that she can't?"

135

Crow turned to look from Henry to Lucien. For an instant Squeaky thought he was going to interrupt. The wretchedness in Lucien's face was now so consuming that he half-thought of intervening himself.

Then Crow leaned back again, saying nothing.

"I bring a different sort of people," Lucien said at last. "People with other tastes: torture, voyeurism, bondage. I didn't bring them enough though. Some things sicken even me. Perhaps if I had brought them, Shadwell wouldn't have killed whoever it was."

"Who was it, Lucien? Niccolo? Rosa? Or Sadie?" Henry asked him.

"I don't know."

"Who is Niccolo?" Squeaky put in. "Did you bring him here?"

"Yes," Lucien said quietly. "Months ago."

"Who is he?" Squeaky insisted.

"A young man with social pretensions," Lucien said with slight contempt. "His father made a lot of money in trade of some sort."

"So why's he here in this gutter, then, not in Society?" Henry said. He glanced to left and right. "This is hardly pretentious."

"You've got to be born into the sort of Society

he's aiming at. You can't buy your way in. I don't know his history, and I don't care." Lucien half-turned away.

Squeaky grabbed Lucien's shoulder and dug his fingers into his flesh.

Lucien winced and cried out.

"Don't you get superior with us, you useless little toad!" Squeaky hissed at him. "Who else've you brought to Shadwell?

"Only those who were more than willing."

This time Lucien was angry.

"Did Niccolo come for drugs, torture, or just women? Sadie in particular?"

"Women," Lucien said. "Sadie wasn't for him."

"Rosa?"

"Yes. He liked Rosa. She was pretty as well, very pretty. But there was a kind of innocence about her, where Sadie could make you believe she knew everything there was to know about pleasure, from the beginning of man and woman—from Eden." For a moment Lucien's memory seemed to drift back into another time.

"Were they on cocaine as well?" Crow asked.

With an effort Lucien forced his attention back to the present. "Who, Rosa? Not so far as I know."

"And Niccolo?"

"Brandy and cocaine."

"From Shadwell?"

"Probably."

"What else did he want from you? What do you do for him that makes you worth his time and his best woman? Sadie was the best woman, wasn't she?" Henry persisted.

"Yes."

"Lucien!"

"He wanted me to bring in better, richer people, friends from my own social class, young men with money who are bored with the tame pleasures of Society." He shrugged very slightly, to avoid causing pain to his wound. "Men who want to escape the predictable, the safe marriage to some nice, tedious young woman and the endless round of the same dinner parties, the same food, and the same conversation for the rest of their lives. They want wild dreams, passion, discovery of new places of the mind, fevers of the imagination and the senses."

"They want the poppy, or cocaine." Henry summed it up. "To give them the dreams they can't create for themselves. Then what are they going to do when they wake up, and all that is left is ashes?"

"Take some more," Lucien said huskily. "I know that. I didn't do what he wanted, which may be why Niccolo might be dead. To teach me the cost of disobedience."

"So Niccolo was dispensable?" Henry asked with a touch of bitterness.

Lucien looked angry, and his expression was answer enough.

Squeaky stood up, his knees creaking. He was cold and sore and so tired he could have slept almost anywhere, except this filthy sty.

"Right. Then we've got to find Niccolo, or Rosa, whichever of them is still alive," he said to all of them. He pointed at Lucien. "You're staying here. You're too sick to be any use, even if we trusted you—which we don't. And someone's got to look after you, which had better be Bessie. You do whatever she says."

He lowered his voice to a grim whisper. "And if you hurt her, or let anyone else hurt her, believe me, you'd rather fall into Shadow Man's hands than mine. He has some use for you, so he probably won't kill you. You're nothing to me, so I'll kill you in a heartbeat—except I won't. I'll do it slow. Got that?"

Lucien smiled, a little crookedly, but there was

warmth to it, no self-pity. "I believe you," he answered. "If Shadwell gets you, which I expect he will, I suppose you expect me to get her back to some kind of world above this one?"

Squeaky was startled. It was the last answer he had looked for. "Yes," he agreed. "That's just what we expect."

Lucien's very quiet laugh ended in a cough. "Poor Bessie. God help her."

Bessie stiffened.

"Never mind God!" Squeaky snapped. "You're all we've got—so you'll do it!"

They bought a good supply of food: mostly bread, cheese, and a little sausage. Henry found enough firewood to keep the stove going, barely, for a couple of days. Crow rebandaged Lucien's wound, then Henry, Squeaky, and Crow left the room quietly and set out on the quest to find Shadwell.

They descended farther into the world of pleasures.

"It's pointless," Squeaky warned. "Even if we find this Shadwell, he can't help Lucien, and he isn't going to try."

He was walking beside Henry as they came to the bottom of a flight of steps and turned left along a passageway with little alleys off to either side. The sound of laughter drifted from the left, along with the smells of wine, smoke, and human sweat, and something else indefinably sickly.

They both stopped.

"This Shadwell isn't keeping Lucien here against his will, you know," Squeaky said to Henry. "Finding him isn't going to do any good."

Henry ignored him, walking again with his hands in his pockets, shoulders hunched. It was bitterly cold down here and they were eager to reach a place crowded with people.

In one of the cellars it was definitely warmer, but the air was so thick with opium fumes it made Henry gag. Even Crow put his scarf around his mouth. In the dim light they saw more than twenty figures sprawled in a mockery of repose. Some seemed conscious, though not fully aware. Their eyes were glazed; they saw nothing of their surroundings, only the hectic world within their own minds.

Henry tried speaking to one or two of them but received no answers of which he could make any sense.

"Don't bother," Squeaky told him. "They wouldn't know their own mothers. Come to think of it, they probably never did. We aren't going to find Shadow Man here. The poppy's his servant, not his master. We'll do better going after the whorehouses. At least the customers will still be conscious."

Crow peered into the faces of some of the smokers. They were mostly men but included a few women. "He's right," he conceded. "This lot can't tell us anything."

They turned to leave, but found their way blocked by a bald-headed man with tattoos on his neck and the parts of his hands that they could see. His right thumb was missing.

"And what would you be doing in 'ere?" he said with a pronounced lisp, as if his tongue were malformed. "Yer lookin' ter come 'ere without payin', then? That ain't the way it works, gents. Yer come in, yer pays."

"We smoke, we pay," Squeaky told him tersely.

"Yer come 'in, yer pays," the man repeated. He jerked his hand sideways sharply and another figure loomed out of the haze to join him.

Henry put his hand into his inside pocket to find money.

"Yer wanna watch 'im!" Squeaky warned, seizing Henry's arm and holding it hard to prevent him from moving. He felt him wince. He would apologize later. Right now he must stop him from revealing that he had any money, or they would all be robbed blind, and lucky to get out uninjured. His instinct was to fight, and they couldn't win. These men would be armed with knives and razors, and possibly garottes as well. Opium was expensive, and therefore worth protecting. Henry had no idea what he was dealing with. With an ounce of a brain Squeaky could have stopped this idiocy before it got this far. He was getting slow, and that was his own fault. He was out of practice. Out of brains, more like.

"'E works for Shadow Man," he said to the others, but nodding his head at Henry. "'E looks like 'e's a gent, and 'e was, once. And them that started as gents, when they hit the gutter, they're worse than them as was born in it. 'E used to be a surgeon. What 'e can do with a knife," he held his finger and thumb a couple of inches apart, "just a little, very, very sharp knife," he said, shuddering, "you wouldn't want to know about."

Henry froze, his jaw dropped in amazement.

Crow smiled, showing all his teeth. "We call him the Bleeder." He caught the spirit of the act. "Looks like butter wouldn't melt, don't he?" He regarded Henry admiringly. "Looks like that until he gets right up close to you. Then it's too late." He raised his right hand so quickly the bald man did not even see it until it was almost at his throat, and then gone again before he could thrust it away.

Crow's smile widened.

"Oh, really!" Henry protested.

Squeaky looked at Henry sternly. "No, Bleeder! Not this time. 'E's only trying it on. 'E don't mean it." He turned to the bald man. "Do you, sir? Say you don't, an' I'll get 'im out of 'ere, no trouble, no blood. Blood's no good for business. People come 'ere for a little peace, a little escape. Blood puts 'em right off."

"Don't you come back, or I'll get you next time!" The bald man said it grimly, but there was no conviction in his voice. He stepped back, leaving them plenty of room.

As one, Crow and Squeaky took Henry by both arms and swung him around. Then they marched him back up the stairs into the alley, right to the far end and out into the narrow square before letting him go.

The fog was growing thicker, and the cobbles were slick with ice. The lamps in the street ahead were almost invisible, little more than smudges against the darkness.

"That was preposterous!" Henry exclaimed, but even in this dim light it was clear to see that he was smiling. "What on earth would you have done if he'd not believed you?"

"Put me fingers in his eyes," Squeaky said without hesitation. "But that could have ended real nasty."

"We'd better keep moving," Crow advised. "We can't afford to have one of that lot catch up with us."

"We want either Rosa or Sadie, whichever of them is alive," Squeaky said. "I'm thinking they aren't bought by just anyone with enough money. I'll wager anything you like that they do the choosing, not the clients, although they might think they do. Shadwell doesn't find their customers for them, they find them for him."

"You're right," Crow agreed. "So how do we get to where they'll find us?"

Squeaky gave him a disparaging look, which was largely wasted because the light was too dim for Crow to see it.

"Yeah? An' which one of us is a woman like

Sadie going to go for, then?" Squeaky asked sarcastically.

"Definitely Crow," Henry replied without hesitation. "You and I are too old, and don't look the part anyway."

Crow's jaw fell. He struggled for words but none came to him. For once even his smile failed him.

Henry patted him on the shoulder. "Your turn," he said cheerfully. "I think we had better fortify ourselves with as good a meal as we can find first. It's going to be a long night."

*A*s it turned out it was two long nights and many wasted attempts before they found the right place—a small, very discreet club where an excellent champagne flowed and both men and women made their availability startlingly plain. There seemed to be endless doors to side rooms, curtains, laughter, farther doors beyond with locks. People wore all kinds of costumes. Some were colorful, even picturesque, borrowed from history or imagination. Others were merely obscene. In some cases it was easy to be deceived as to whether the wearer was male or female. Some appeared to have bosoms and yet also wore large and very suggestive codpieces.

Almost every distortion of appetite was catered to. Two or even three men together was illegal, but commonplace enough here. A near-naked hermaphrodite, clearly possessing rudimentary organs of both sexes, turned even Squeaky's stomach.

A slim, pale boy offered himself for sexual asphyxiation, and Henry averted his eyes, his face white. Squeaky wondered how long it would be before someone lost control and the boy ended up dead.

"Would you fancy something to eat, gentlemen?" another young man asked. "What's your pleasure, sirs? Oysters to spark the appetite a little? Champagne? Chocolate, perhaps? Soft, dark chocolate to lick off a woman's body?" He giggled. "Or a man's if you prefer? Got a nice young boy that nature was generous to . . ."

For once Henry was lost for a reply.

Crow shook his head.

"We'll find our own!" Squeaky snapped, surprised to hear how hoarse his voice was. "Don't worry—we'll pay."

The man swiveled on his heel and went off in a pettish temper.

Squeaky looked at Henry's too-evident distress.

"Take that look off your face!" he hissed, digging his elbow sharply into Henry's ribs. "Yer look like you just bit into a rotten egg."

"I feel like it," Henry said, gasping and coughing. "What in God's name has happened to these people?"

"How the hell do I know? Look, I never dealt in this kind of thing!" He was indignant now. Did Henry really think this was commonplace to him? "What kind of a . . ."

Henry shook his head. "The question was rhetorical."

"What?" Squeaky was hurt.

"A question that does not expect an answer," Henry explained. "I don't really imagine that you know, any more than I do, what creates this out of people who must once have been . . . normal."

"Oh." Squeaky was relieved. A heavy, stifling weight had been lifted from him.

He was straightening his jacket and beginning to look around him when he saw her. She was standing almost ten feet away from them, leaning slightly backward against one of the pillars that held up the ceiling. It was not her laughter that had caught his attention, or any movement of the man facing her, it was the extraordinary grace of her body. Her face was lifted to look at the man, her profile delicate, her long white throat smoothly curved. Her hair was jet-black and her lips artificially red. She was the only person in the noisy, hysterical room who was absolutely motionless. And yet her very stillness was more alive than any action of the rest of them. It was Sadie. It had to be. Which meant Rosa was dead—or Niccolo.

"Crow!" he hissed urgently. "Crow!"

Henry looked at him, then turned to Crow, touching him on the arm.

Crow swung around, then froze. His eyes widened.

"Go on," Henry urged. "Now."

"But she's . . ." Crow protested.

"We've got no time to waste," Henry told him. "Do it now, or I'll have to."

Crow hesitated.

Squeaky moved behind him and gave him a hard shove in the middle of his back.

Crow shot forward with a yelp and stopped a yard short of Sadie.

She looked at him, smiling with amusement. "That's original—even inventive." She looked him up and down, quite openly appraising him.

The young man she had been speaking to snatched Crow's arm hot-temperedly and said something almost unintelligible to Squeaky, who was watching.

Henry was clearly anxious. He started to intervene.

"No!" Squeaky said sharply. "Leave him!"

Crow gave the young man a dazzling smile, all white teeth and wide-open eyes. Then he kicked him very hard in one shin. The young man howled with anger and surprise. Crow seized Sadie and marched her away to a moderately empty space hard up against the wall.

Henry and Squeaky followed almost on her heels.

"They're my friends," Crow explained simply. "We need to talk to you," he added.

"You're Sadie?"

She nodded.

Sadie was amused. Crow was unusual-looking—not unattractive, just eccentric. Perhaps that appealed to Sadie more than the typical spoiled and demanding sort of young man who frequented such places. Also, he was sober and did not have the faded, rather pasty look of so many of the other inhabitants of the night world of the West End.

Sadie raised her elegant eyebrows. "Really? About what?"

"About Lucien Wentworth," Henry replied.

Sadie's smile froze.

Squeaky moved around to stand closer to her to block her retreat. At this particular moment the dim lighting of the room was an advantage; even the crowding helped. They could hear from the distance cries and moans of all sorts, raw farmyard emotions under the gaudy paint of sophistication.

"He's . . . dead," she said, her voice faltering.

"No, he isn't, any more than you are," Squeaky snapped. "It was Niccolo or Rosa who was murdered, and you know that. Maybe both. Lot of blood on the ground. Who was it, Sadie, and why?"

She kept her face toward Henry, as if he were the one most likely to believe her lies. "I don't know. I didn't kill anyone."

"You may not have held the knife," Henry agreed. "But you sharpened it, and gave it to someone. Who? And why?"

She swallowed. The pallor of her skin was almost ghostly in the subterranean light. Her eyes were brilliant, very wide, with black lashes. There was a feline grace to the way she held her body.

Her beauty was strangely disturbing, but there was something ephemeral about it.

"I don't know what you're talking about!" she said angrily. "If somebody's dead, it's nothing to do with me."

"That's a clumsy lie," Henry told her. "You don't survive here not knowing who's been murdered, and why. If it was Niccolo, then you've lost a lover. If it was Rosa, then it could be you next."

She stared at him with venom naked in her eyes. "You bastard!" she said between clenched teeth. "You touch me and I'll make you pay for it in ways you can't even imagine. You'll wish someone would put a knife to your throat—quickly!"

"Is that what it was?" Henry asked, his expression barely changing. "Revenge? Discipline for taking something that belonged to you, perhaps?"

She looked harder at his face, and saw in it something she did not recognize. Perhaps it stirred in her a memory of some better time.

"I didn't kill anyone," she said, still between her teeth, but more slowly, as if she was now afraid.

"But you know who did, because you led them to it, didn't you?"

She shook her head and made short, jerky movements of denial with her hands.

"I couldn't help it! I have to do what he tells me, or . . . or he won't give me any more cocaine, and I'll die." Something in her hectic eyes brought back to Squeaky's memory the first brothel he had ever been in. He had been almost six, taken there by his mother, told to start work on cleaning up behind the customers, sweeping, washing, always being polite to people. "They put the bread on your plate," she had told him. "Don't you ever forget that, boy."

There had been a young girl there then, for her first time. He could recall the smell of sweat and blood and fear, no matter how hard he tried to forget it. And he had tried. He had filled his mind with a thousand other things: his own pleasures in women, some of whom he had even liked, victories won over men he hated, good food, good wine, warmth, the touch of silk. But he could still smell that fear sometimes, alone in the middle of the night.

"Then you'll lead us to him now," Henry said to Sadie, his voice breaking the spell in Squeaky's head and forcing him back to the present.

"He won't help you. Leave him alone."

Crow moved slightly. Squeaky saw the distress in his face, which was composed of embarrassment, revulsion, and an anger within himself that he could do nothing to control.

"I don't believe it's got anything to do with Shadwell," Crow said deliberately. "You killed Rosa and Niccolo. I don't know how. Maybe you killed Niccolo first. You could have held him in your arms, and put a knife in his back, then cut his throat. You lured Rosa there, and when she was stunned at what she saw, you used the knife again. Perhaps she bent over Niccolo's body, maybe weeping. It wouldn't be hard for you to come at her from behind. One single slice from one ear—"

"I didn't!" Sadie cried, lunging forward as if to scratch at his face, everything in her changing from the pleading to the attack.

Squeaky grabbed her, pinning her arms to her sides. She struggled, and she had the strength of desperation. He kicked her hard and her legs collapsed under her, pitching her forward.

Henry was startled and profoundly disconcerted. He bent forward to help her up. "I think you had better take me to Shadwell," he said clearly. "See what he has to say about it."

She surrendered with startling suddenness, as if all her strength had bled away.

Squeaky knew better than to trust her this time. He stood well back, watching, ready to move quickly if she changed her mind.

"I'll take you," she said, and turned and led them out of the hall, then along one passage after another, and down several flights of steps. It was damp and bitingly cold. The air smelled stale, and there was something on the walls that could have been mold.

Then Sadie seemed to change her mind. Almost doubling back on herself, she climbed a long, narrow flight of stairs upward.

"Where the devil are we going?" Squeaky demanded as they came outside into the night and followed her across a lantern-lit, freezing yard. The wind groaned in the eaves of the high buildings crowding around the small space. There were icicles hanging from broken gutters, and a rat scrabbled its way, burrowing among the discarded refuse for food.

Sadie avoided a wide door that looked as if it might have led to a tavern, and instead went to a narrow, poky opening between one stone wall and another. She turned sideways to get through the opening, and for a moment Squeaky was afraid she had escaped them.

He pushed his way through ahead of Henry and Crow. He felt in his pocket for his knife in case he should need it as soon as he emerged.

But there was only Sadie waiting for him. As soon as she saw him she started to walk away, knowing he would follow her. He looked at the pale gleam of her skin above her dress and wondered how she didn't perish with the cold. Then an uglier thought occurred to him: Perhaps, in all senses that mattered, she was in a way dead already. He had seen a despair in her eyes that made that easy to believe.

Were they fools to follow her into this deeper hell than the wild self-indulgence they had already seen? How could he persuade Henry Rathbone not to go with her, when they seemed so close to finding Shadwell, and perhaps enough of the truth to convince Lucien to come back into the warm, breathing world and pay whatever it would cost him to go home again?

Squeaky was disgusted with himself that he liked Henry so much. What use was liking someone? It only ever got you into trouble. And if he imagined that they would like him in return, then he was stupider than the most idiotic drunkard in the halls and taverns they had just left. When this was over, Henry Rathbone would go back to his safe, clean house on Primrose Hill, and Squeaky would go back to keeping the books for Hester in the clinic on Portpool Lane. It would be surprising if they ever met again. Squeaky would have sacrificed his own internal comfort for nothing at all.

At the far end of the alley Sadie led them into another open patch where there was a narrow, scarred door. She pulled a key from around her neck and opened the lock, closing it behind them again when they were inside.

Here a wider stair led down into a labyrinth. They heard laughter, the drip and gurgle of water, and voices that echoed along the tunnels through which she walked as surely as if the way were marked before her.

Squeaky tried at first to keep track of where they were going—left or right, up or down— but after a quarter of an hour he knew he was lost. He was not even sure how far below the surface they were. He began to feel steadily worse about the whole thing. What had happened to the sense that usually warned him of danger? Except that he knew perfectly well what had happened to it: He had let it slip away from him because he was a fool, wanting to be liked.

He caught up with Sadie and grasped her arm. She stopped abruptly.

"Where are we?" he demanded. "You've taken us round in circles! Where's Shadwell, then?" He held her hard, deliberately pinching the flesh of her arm.

She did not pull away, as if she barely felt it. "Not far," she answered. "I'll show you where he is, then I'll . . ."

There was the noise of a door slamming not far from them, and then soft laughter.

Squeaky froze. He swore vehemently under his breath, then looked across at Crow a yard away from him. Even in the half-light he could see the fear in his face. Beyond him, Henry was little more than a shadow.

Sadie turned to Crow. "He knows we're here," she whispered. "I thought I would trick him coming this way, but he still knows. We've got to get out. Come back another time."

"What does he do down here?" Squeaky demanded.

"We're not that far down," Sadie replied. She was shivering. "Tell me where you want to go and I'll take you there. You can come back for Shadwell any time." She took the key off the chain around her neck and passed it to him. Her sea-blue eyes were almost luminous in the gleam. "Where do you want to get out?"

Crow named an alley. It was quarter of a mile from the room where they had left Lucien and Bessie, but a tortuous and half-hidden route.

Sadie nodded. "Follow me." There was urgency in her voice now, and an edge of fear that had not been there before. "It isn't very far."

They obeyed. Squeaky glanced at Crow and knew that he would be trying to remember it as well.

She had not lied to them. It was perhaps twenty minutes later when they stood outside in the alley. The wind had dropped, and the fog was thick, so that it lay in a blanket over the roofs and trailed long, white fingers of blindness in the streets.

They parted from Sadie, and she was lost to their sight within moments. Crow crept forward, leading the way. He knew it well enough, even in this sightless condition.

Lucien and Bessie were waiting for them. Lucien was sitting up now and had a little color in his face.

"D'yer find 'im?" Bessie asked eagerly. She sat on the floor close to Lucien. There were several pieces of bread on an old newspaper, and the stove was still just alight. She gave them each a portion of bread, taking the smallest for herself. There was cheese also, but she gave all of it to Lucien. Squeaky wondered how many women she had seen do that for those they cared for, saying nothing of it, pretending they had already eaten their share.

"We know where he is," Henry told her.

Squeaky was less sure, but he chose not to argue.

Henry recounted to Lucien their finding of Sadie, and her story that she had had no part in killing either Rosa or Niccolo.

Squeaky watched Lucien's face, judging whether he knew all this: if it were lies, or the truth.

"Oh, just tell my father you couldn't find me," Lucien said to Henry. "For the person he wants you to find, that's true enough. You won't be lying."

"Yes 'e would," Bessie spoke suddenly. "'Cause you're lyin'." She looked at Henry. "Did 'is Pa say as 'e 'ad ter be a certain kind o' person, or did 'e just say 'is son?"

"He just said his son," Henry replied. He looked again at Lucien. "I did not imagine it would be easy for you. You do not simply walk away from people such as these. And before you leave, you have to prove that you did not kill Niccolo, or Rosa. You have to prove it to the people who cared for them, and you have to prove it to us. If you don't, it is going to haunt you for the rest of your life, quite possibly in the very unpleasant form of someone coming after you. Surely you are not foolish enough to imagine that going back to your home would put you beyond their reach?"

"No," Lucien agreed. "There is no such place of safety. There is always somebody who can be bought, whether for simple money, or from hunger of one sort or another—or out of fear."

Bessie was looking at him, chewing her lower lip, waiting to see what he would do.

"They don't know where you are," Squeaky put in. "We'll go and find him tomorrow."

Lucien hitched himself up on his elbow.

"Not you," Squeaky told him sharply. "You're not well enough. You'll just get in the way."

"But . . ."

"You'll stay here with Bessie. We haven't got time to be looking out for you. Do as you're told, unless you want me to set that wound of yours back a few days?"

Lucien met his eyes steadily for several seconds, then lowered his gaze and lay back again.

Bessie kept looking at Squeaky, trying to work out in her mind what he meant, and if he would really have hurt Lucien again. Squeaky turned away. He did not want to know what answer she reached.

A few hours later Henry, Crow, and Squeaky set out again, this time to find Shadwell without Sadie's help—or presence to warn him. Bessie and Lucien were both asleep, and they did not disturb them. There was really no need.

It was a short journey back through the streets to where Sadie had left them, counted in paces through the all-enveloping fog. They returned the way they had come, and used the key to the door that led downward toward where she had said Shadow Man would be.

"What are you going to say to him, if he's there?" Crow asked.

Squeaky looked at Henry expectantly.

"A devil's deal," Henry answered quietly. "But

one that will prove to Ash, and his friends, that Lucien did not kill Rosa."

"Or Niccolo?" Crow asked. "Doesn't it matter about him?"

"No, not much," Henry said, moving forward carefully on the slick stones. "I think we might find that Niccolo is still alive."

"There was a lot of blood for one person," Crow said unhappily. "If the second body wasn't Niccolo, who was it?"

"If I'm right, I'll explain. For now we haven't time for a lot of talking." Henry led the way down the steps and along the stone corridor.

Squeaky looked at Crow and saw the anxiety in his face. They both hesitated.

Squeaky swore. "Come on! If we don't go with him, the damn fool will go alone. Anything could happen to him. Why do I always meet up with such idiots?" He hurried and nearly missed his step on the uneven surface. Crow strode behind him. There was no sound but the scraping of their boots on the stone and the steady dripping of water.

The words "a devil's deal" kept going around in Squeaky's head. What had Henry Rathbone meant? He wanted to ask now, but it took all his concentration to keep up with Henry and Crow in these miserable winding passages.

Then suddenly he recognized a stairway up to their left, and in front of them a door with a brass handle.

"We're in the wrong place!" he said simply, catching Henry by the arm. "This is the room of that fearful little creature in the velvet coat."

"I know," Henry answered. "The man who knows exactly what happened to Rosa, I believe."

"He killed her? Why? What did she . . ."

"No. He didn't kill her, but I think he knows who did."

"Why didn't he tell us?" With every new turn of events Squeaky was beginning to feel worse and worse about this whole idea of coming back.

"Because he wants to take revenge himself on the man who did," Henry answered quietly.

"Why?" Squeaky asked. "What's Rosa to him?"

"Doctor Crow?" Henry prompted.

"I think she's his daughter," Crow answered gently.

"What? How d'you know that?" Squeaky was aghast.

"Do you remember Lucien saying that Rosa had unusual eyes?" Crow asked. "One hazel and one green?"

"Yes. What about it?"

"I asked someone else and they said the same thing . . ."

"So what does that matter?" Squeaky was growing impatient. "Are you saying that it wasn't Rosa who was dead, then? So who was it?"

"Yes, I think it was Rosa," Crow replied.

"The color of your eyes is something that doesn't change with age, except perhaps to fade a bit," Henry interrupted. "If you think back, you'll remember that Ash had odd eyes too. What do you think the chances are that they are closely related to each other?"

Squeaky let out his breath in a long sigh. "Yeah. I never saw that. So what's your devil's deal?"

Henry took a long, slow breath. "A Christian burial for Rosa, if Ash will admit that the second body was Niccolo, and that he killed him in revenge for his murdering Rosa."

"Are you sure he did?" Squeaky asked.

"No, I just think so. It makes sense. Who else would?" Henry asked. "Perhaps he didn't mean to,

165

just lost his temper. Apparently he was violent. Maybe he was wild on withdrawal from cocaine. No one had seen him since her death."

"You mean you believe Lucien that he didn't do it," Squeaky concluded, not sure if he was pleased, frightened, disgusted, or maybe all three. He had not felt so confused in years, maybe not ever. He could not afford all this . . . feeling.

"Do you know of some reason I should not?" Henry said.

Squeaky swore vehemently and from the heart. "'Cause it's bloody stupid! It's dangerous," he hissed. He wanted to shout at Henry, but he could not afford to make such a noise right outside Ash's rooms. "You can't go around just believing anything anyone wants to tell you! You could get taken—"

"I said 'reason,'" Henry corrected him gently. "Not fear."

"Fear's a reason!" Squeaky was exasperated. "It's one of the best reasons I know. It's kept me alive, with my skin whole, for fifty bleedin' years!"

"And has it made you happy, Squeaky?"

"Yes!" He waved his hand in a gesture of denial. "No! Well—I'm alive, and you don't get very happy dead! What a question to ask!"

"You don't have to come and see Ash if you'd rather not," Henry told him.

That was the final insult. "You trying to say you don't want me?" Squeaky demanded. This hurt, badly.

"Not at all." Henry smiled and took Squeaky's arm. He turned to Crow. "Come, Dr. Crow, let us see if the poor man will accept our deal."

Our deal? Ours? Squeaky was about to protest, then realized he really wanted to be included. He banged on the door and then threw it open.

The room inside was empty. Squeaky was crushed with disappointment.

"We'll wait," Henry decided. "At least for a while." He sat down on the filthy floor.

They had not long to sit. When Ash returned he was still wearing the absurd lavender coat. His face seemed even more gaunt, the white painted skin stretched over the bones of his skull. He used the stick to prod the ground, as if he were not certain that it was firm enough to hold his weight.

"Well!" he said with interest. "And what do you want this time? You found Lucien. And Sadie." He said her name slowly, as if it hurt him.

"Indeed," Henry replied. "But we did not find Rosa or Niccolo. I think you could help us with that."

Squeaky looked at the terrible face, which was like a chalk mask. Crow was right; one of his eyes was hazel, the other quite definitely green. Perhaps Henry was right too that Rosa was this man's daughter. It made a sort of tragic sense.

Ash stood motionless as a garish figurine.

"In order to give them a Christian burial," Henry went on. "Or Rosa, at least. Perhaps Niccolo doesn't deserve one. They don't do that for men they hang."

Ash smiled. It was sad and horrible. "He wasn't hanged. Not strong enough to lift him, you see." He raised his hands, but stiffly, as if they would not go higher than his shoulders.

"How did you kill him?" Henry inquired as if it were no more than a matter of courteous interest.

Ash tapped his stick with his other hand. "Dagger in here," he replied. "Very useful. Had a proper sword once. Haven't the balance to hold it anymore now. Dagger will do. He didn't even see me. Just killed my beautiful Rosa. I put the blade through his heart. I was surprised how much he bled."

"He probably took a little while to die," Crow observed. "People don't bleed much after they're dead."

"Really?" Ash looked only mildly interested. "A Christian burial? Why?"

"Because I want something from you," Henry replied. "Of course."

"What?"

"That you tell people the truth, so Lucien is not blamed for either death."

"And you'll bury Rosa, decently, like a Christian?"

"I will."

"Where is she?" Henry said wearily.

Without speaking again Ash turned, leaning awkwardly on his stick, and led them out of the room. In the passage he started in the opposite direction from the one they had taken before. After a hundred feet or so they went into a small side room, cold and dry, where two bodies lay side by side on a table. One was a young woman, her long dark hair loose around her face, her hands folded as if totally at peace. Her eyes were closed. Even so, her features were a finer, almost beautiful echo of what Ash's might have been in his youth, before disease spoiled them.

Her dress was matted with blood where someone had stabbed her over and over.

The man, by contrast, bore only one wound, to the heart. His arms were by his sides.

They stood in a few moments' respectful silence. It was Crow who broke it.

"I'll carry her," he said quietly. "Do you have a cloth of any kind to wrap around her?"

❖

*W*hen they were far beyond the hall and heading toward the way up, they came face-to-face with Sadie, and behind her Lucien and Bessie.

Henry stopped instantly, Squeaky, Crow, and Ash close on his heels. One glance at Henry's face was enough to show that he did not understand, but Squeaky did. It was all now horribly clear. Sadie had been so eager to help because she needed to see where they were keeping Lucien. Now she had gone back to collect him—for Shadwell! Always his servant, bought and paid for with the cocaine she could or would not live without.

Bessie had come as well, either with them or close after. Her ridiculous sense of loyalty would make her do that. Now they were all trapped. He

170

didn't even need to turn around to know that the way would be closed behind them.

Shadwell was there in the half-light, as Squeaky had known he would be. He did not even notice if he was tall or short, except that he wore a frock coat, like an undertaker. It was his face that dominated everything else, every thought and emotion. The lantern on the wall threw his left side into high relief, illuminating the bony nose and sunken cheekbones, the wide, cruel lips. The darker side was only half visible, the eye socket lost, the bones merely suggested, the mouth a shapeless slash on the skin.

There was an instant's utter silence, then Henry spoke.

"Mr. Shadwell, I presume?" he said quietly. His voice was absurdly polite, and shaking only a very little.

Shadwell remained motionless where he was. "And you, sir, must be Henry Rathbone." His reply was almost gentle. As Sadie had said, it was a voice that crept inside the head and remained there.

"I am," Henry agreed. "We would be obliged if you would allow us to pass. We are taking the body of Rosa in order to give her burial."

"Ah, yes, Rosa." The man let her name roll on his tongue. "What an unfortunate waste. She was hardly Sadie, but she was still worth something. By all means bury her. Put a Christian cross above her empty soul, if it gives you some sense of your own worthiness. It will fool neither God nor Satan."

Squeaky gulped. He wished Ash had not had to hear that.

"All obsequies for the dead are to preserve our own humanity," Henry answered him. "Reminders of who we are, and that we loved them. The present is woven out of the threads of the past."

Shadwell inclined his head a little, allowing the light to shine on his face, making it look worse. "A silken rope to bind you," he agreed. "I will let the good doctor go, taking Rosa. The rest of you stay. I dare say in time I shall find a use for you."

"And Lucien," Henry added.

"And Bessie!" Squeaky insisted. How could Henry forget her?

"You make a hard bargain," Shadwell responded. "What do you think, Sadie? Could you teach this bony child to be a good whore?"

Squeaky looked at Sadie. Her face should have been beautiful, but now there was an ugliness inside her that soured it.

It was Lucien who moved. He stepped toward Shadwell, his head high, his arms held a little forward, still protecting his wound.

"I'll stay. I'll do whatever you need, even bring in men from my own society who want to come, if you let all these go, including Bessie. I'm of far more use to you than she'll ever be. She doesn't know or care how to please men. She has no art at all." He stood a little straighter, his eyes never leaving Shadwell's. His face was yellowish gray in the sullen light.

Shadwell's eyes widened, like sunken pits in his skull. "You trust my word?" he asked incredulously.

Lucien tried to smile, and failed. He was shaking. "Of course not. I shall bring to you every greedy and twisted man who can pay you, for as long as I know they are safe, including Bessie."

"Indeed. Or you'll do what? Are you threatening me?"

"Or I will kill myself," Lucien said simply. "I am no use to you dead, but alive and willing, I can bring men—and more women as lush as Sadie."

A look of anger and surprise filled Shadwell's terrible face.

Lucien had won the bargain, at least for the

moment. He knew it. His skin was ashen. He was entering a real hell: one that he understood intimately, could taste on his tongue and in his throat, and one that would never leave him.

Henry Rathbone was smiling, and tears welled up in his eyes. He watched and said nothing. That was when Squeaky knew that, for him, Lucien had redeemed himself.

Henry took Squeaky by the arm very firmly, so that his fingers dug into Squeaky's flesh, and pulled him away.

Bessie was on Squeaky's heels. Crow followed, still carrying Rosa's body. Ash was nowhere to be seen.

They walked as quickly as they could along the tunnels and passages, and up the flight of steps, slippery underfoot, lit only by a couple of rush torches soaked in pitch.

Bessie pulled so hard on the tails of Squeaky's jacket she very nearly tore the fabric. He stopped and whirled around on her, then did not know what to say.

Behind him Crow stopped as well, leaning against the wall, breathing hard. He carefully allowed the weight of Rosa's body to rest on the ground.

"We in't goin' ter leave 'im, are we?" Bessie said, her voice trembling.

"No," Henry answered her. "But we must think very carefully what we are going to do, and how. I think we are far enough away to take a rest. And we must keep our promise to Ash, wherever he has got to."

"'Im?" she said in disbelief. "'E's a—"

"It is our promise, not his," Henry reminded her. "But quite apart from that, he did keep his bargain."

"So where is 'e then?" she demanded.

"Probably watching us, to see if we keep our part," Crow said wryly. "He doesn't know you as well as we do."

Henry gave him a quick smile. Squeaky thought of all the sane, sensible people above them in the daylight, preparing for Christmas, buying gifts, getting geese ready to roast, mixing pastries and puddings and cakes. He could almost smell the sweetness of it. There would be wreaths of holly on doors, music in the air. Sometime soon there would even be bells. These people knew what Christmas was supposed to be.

"But we're going back for Lucien?" Bessie insisted.

"Of course we are," Henry assured her. "But we must do it with a plan. We have no weapons, so we have to think very carefully. Crow, you had better take Rosa's body somewhere safe, where it can come to no possible harm, and where we can be sure it will be given a Christian burial, should we find ourselves in a position where we cannot attend to that ourselves."

"You mean if we're dead!" Squeaky snapped.

"I would prefer not to have put it so crudely, but yes," Henry agreed. Then he turned back to Crow. "Do you know of such a place? Perhaps friends who owe you a favor? I am willing to pay; that is not an issue. I will write an I.O.U. that my son will honor, should that become necessary. Surely in your professional capacity you are acquainted with undertakers?"

Crow smiled, almost a baring of his teeth. "A few. It will take me at least half an hour to see to it."

"Then you had better begin," Henry urged. "In the meantime we will consider what weapon we can create that will be of use to us in battle against Shadow Man."

Crow picked up Rosa's body again. He staggered a little under her weight, although she was slight.

Squeaky realized how far he had carried her already, without a word of complaint or the request that someone else take a turn.

"We need a good weapon," he said unhappily, although a fearful idea was beginning to take shape in his mind. He did not want to look at it, not even for an instant, but it was there, undeniable.

"Crow!" he shouted.

Crow stopped. He was almost at the next bend in the passage. "What?"

"Bring some matches," Squeaky called. "Lots of them."

Henry stared at him. "Fire?" he said hoarsely. "For God's sake, Squeaky, we don't know anything about the airflow down here, or which tunnels lead to which others. We could end up killing everyone." His voice cracked. "We could end up setting fire to half of London!"

"I'll bet that little bastard Ash knows," Squeaky said darkly. "You shouldn't have let Crow take the girl's body. You gave away the one thing we could have bargained with." How could Henry be so clever and so stupid? Squeaky would never understand some people.

"We already used it," Henry pointed out.

"Well, we could've used it again, if you hadn't let Crow take her!" Squeaky protested.

"No, I couldn't. Quite apart from the morality of it, it isn't very wise." Henry smiled. "How can a man trust me if I've already cheated him once?"

Squeaky was obliged to concede that there was a certain logic in that. "Do you wish me to go and look for the little swine?" he offered.

"There is no point. You won't find him if he doesn't want you to."

Squeaky swore. He really needed more words if he was going to continue in Henry Rathbone's acquaintance. Everything he knew was insufficient to express the pent-up emotions inside him, the rage, the pity, the sheer, blind frustration of it all. Not to mention the fear!

There was a tiny sound behind him and he swung around. Ash was standing no more than a couple of yards away.

"Don't creep up on people!" Squeaky shouted at him. "You could get yourself killed like that."

Ash looked at him in disdain. "Not until after you've killed Shadwell," he replied. "You need me until then."

Henry looked at him. "We don't intend to kill

Shadwell, just to rescue Lucien, and Sadie if she wishes it."

Ash leaned on his cane. Henry offered him a hand to steady himself and he took it, reluctantly. "Same thing," he said. "He won't give up, and he knows these tunnels and passages far better than you do."

"Then you are quite right when you say that we need your help," Henry agreed. "We need to have some form of plan by the time Dr. Crow returns. He has gone to take Rosa's body to where it will be safe, and buried properly, if we find that we cannot do it ourselves."

"I know."

Henry opened his mouth to say something, then changed his mind. "Do you know these passages well enough to help us?" he said instead.

"Of course I do," the man replied. "What is your plan?"

Henry smiled ruefully. "We have very little yet. We wish to rescue Lucien and Sadie, and prevent Shadwell from following us out. The only weapon we have is fire."

Ash pulled his grotesque face into an even more bizarre grimace. "Then we must get Lucien out.

We can set fires that will trap Shadwell so that he cannot follow you. Sadie will not come. Lucien may. You must be prepared for any answer, and willing to leave them, or you will be burned as well."

"We know," Henry agreed.

Henry dug around in his pockets and found a piece of paper on which Ash could draw a plan of the tunnels, steps, and passages through buildings where Shadwell would likely be, along with the direction of drafts, and so the way fire would travel.

"We'll have to wall him in," Ash explained. "Here." He pointed to the end of a network of pathways.

"Doesn't he have an escape door, a back way out?" Squeaky asked. "I would."

Ash smiled. "That way." He put his fingers carefully on the paper. "Into the sewers."

"As long as we get Lucien," Henry said quietly, his face pale. "We may have to forgo getting Shadwell too."

Ash touched the paper again. "If we set fires here, and here, and maybe here, too, then we've got him. You'll need to collect as much rubbish as you can, stuff that'll burn easy." He smiled. There was something ghastly about it, and Squeaky found himself turning away from the sight. "I know where they keep the oil for the lamps," Ash went on. "And the tar for the torches along the tunnels where they can use a flame. We'll have a fire to make hell proud."

*B*y the time Crow returned they had collected oil, tar, several piles of tallow candles, and as much old wood and rags as they could find without robbing people whose attention they could not afford to attract.

They crept forward together. Ash led the way, tapping his stick on the ground to make certain of it so his nerve-dead feet did not trip him. He was followed by Henry, Crow, Bessie, and Squeaky, all carrying or dragging behind them roughly made sacks of candles, pieces of wood, tins, bottles, and jugs of oil, and buckets of tar. When they reached the places the man showed them, they very carefully laid their fires, sometimes with a fuse made of torn and knitted rags soaked in oil, aided by a little tar. There was no time for error or for waiting and watching.

With shaking hands Squeaky lit a match, held it as still as his trembling hands would allow, then touched it to the rags. It ignited immediately. The flame raced along it and caught hold. He jerked back, watched it for another moment to make sure it was not going to die, then ran as fast as he could to the second site to set it burning too.

He knew Crow was doing the same with the other fires.

Henry, Bessie, and Ash made their way to the heart of Shadwell's territory, expecting to meet him around every corner or through every door or archway.

When they finally did, it was deeper than they had been before. They crossed a last threshold into a clean, stark cellar with doorways to both the right and left, and one to the back. The last must lead to the sewer, the other to the tunnel where the fire was already approaching. Shadwell was sitting in an armchair with Lucien in a chair opposite him. Sadie stood casually by a table with a cabinet next to it, filled with tiny carved wooden drawers.

"What now?" Shadwell asked, rising to his feet. "Have you changed your mind? Come to give me the girl and take Lucien in exchange? I'm afraid you cannot do that. You see, Lucien is right. He is of far more use to me than she could ever be. You made your bargain and it stands."

"I came back to ask Lucien if he wishes to leave," Henry replied. "You too, for that matter. Although I have no idea where you might go. I doubt there is a place for you above the ground."

For several seconds Shadwell did not reply.

"You are right." His voice was still very quiet, insistent, and the strange sibilance was even more pronounced. "My place is here, in all the stairways and passages that thread under the blind, busy world. This is my world. But you chose to come into it. Everyone who is here chose to be, but I choose who stays and who leaves. I let you leave once, but not this time."

Crow came up behind Henry. Squeaky appeared at his other side, but facing backward, keeping guard over the tunnel.

"Go, while you can!" Lucien said urgently. "He's right. I made my decision and I'll abide by it."

Henry could smell smoke drifting toward them from the passage beyond Squeaky: a sharp, acrid stinging in his nose. In another moment they would all be aware of it. And the flames could not be far behind if the man in lavender was right about the flow of air in the tunnels.

"Lucien!" Henry said urgently.

Lucien shook his head. "Let me pay my debts," he answered gravely. "Please tell my father that I did that. Go, while you can. You don't owe me anything. You never did."

The smoke was getting stronger. Suddenly Shadwell caught the odor of it. His eyes widened and his head jerked higher. The only way of escape was either past Henry, Crow, and Squeaky, or past Lucien through the door behind them, into the sewers.

The crackle of fire was audible now.

It was Bessie who broke the silence. She walked forward to Lucien, past the line of the door to the left. "Lucien, yer gotta come wi' us. Squeaky and me come back for yer. Yer can't stay 'ere . . ."

The door to the left crashed in and the fire spread across the room, cutting them off with a wall of heat.

"Bessie!" Squeaky cried out desperately. "Yer stupid little cow! What . . . Oh, God!" He tore off his jacket and put it half across his head, then bent and charged through the flames to where he could still just see her. The heat was terrible, but he was through the wall and out the other side to find Bessie gripping Lucien's arm.

She swung around.

Squeaky seized her, picking her up. She weighed almost nothing. He could feel her bones through the thin cloth of her dress. He turned, but the fire was taking hold. It was hotter, spreading already. He hesitated. How could he get her back through it to the way out? What if her clothes caught fire? Her hair?

There was no time to even think. He put his head down and charged. He felt the flames all around him for a terrifying moment. The pain was enough to make him cry out, but he bit it back, afraid to draw in a scorching breath.

Then he was out the other side, Bessie still in his arms. Crow clutched hold of him, throwing his coat over Bessie and holding it, smothering the flames that licked at her dress.

No one had noticed Henry going the other way through the flames toward Lucien, Sadie, and Shadwell.

Lucien stared at him, horrified. "You can't come with us!" he said urgently, his eyes flickering just once toward the doorway to the sewers.

"I don't intend to," Henry replied. "But if you hurry, you can come with me. There's still time to get back through the fire, if we go now."

But it was Shadwell who answered. "You want him, you must pay." He was standing close to Sadie, between her and Henry. He put out his hand and his strong, heavy fingers closed like a vise on arm. "If he goes with you, I will kill her."

Henry hesitated.

"Slowly," Shadwell elaborated. "Painfully."

"You are doing that already," Henry told him. "My leaving Lucien behind will not change that. As you have pointed out before, those who are with you are there by choice. I don't know what choices Sadie has left. Each decision we take can narrow them. But if she will not fight to save herself, no one else can do it. There comes a point when we all stand alone."

Lucien took a step toward them.

"Go, while you can," Henry ordered him. "I'm coming with you." He turned, and in that instant Shadwell let go of Sadie and put his other hand on Henry. His grip was like iron. For a moment, as he saw Lucien step into the flames, Henry was paralyzed. The pain in his arm took his breath away.

Lucien was gone. Sadie was still standing by the wall, stunned.

Henry swung around to face Shadwell. He had never physically fought anyone in his life. There was only instinct to prompt him.

Shadwell's face was close to his. For the first time in the red light of the flames, Henry saw his eyes, empty keyholes into hell in his uneven face. He could not bear to look at them. He bent forward a little and charged, knocking them both off balance and toppling onto the floor, kicking at each other. It was ridiculous and desperate. The heat was filling the room and sucking the air out of it. Henry was gasping already.

Shadwell was on top of him, holding his throat. He couldn't breathe at all. The room swam into darkness.

Then suddenly he was slapped, hard, and gasped for air.

"Get up!" a voice hissed at him. "Get up, you fool! Take my arm!"

Henry opened his eyes, expecting to see Crow and Squeaky, but it was Ash hitting him with the little strength he had. "Get out of here, down the sewer and turn left. Stay left at every turn. Go!"

Henry struggled to his knees. The fire all but filled the room now. Shadwell was on the floor, kneeling, rising, his back to the flames. Sadie was screaming, her clothes alight. Henry tried to lunge toward her but Ash kicked him in the ribs. Henry doubled up with the pain of it and found himself staggering forward. A hard shove from behind and he was through the open doorway. It slammed shut behind him. In seconds the room would be an inferno. Yet he was safe and utterly alone, unable to go back, unable to help.

The sour smell of the sewers was cold and damp, a balm to his seared skin. He was glad to step into the icy water and wade to the left. Feeling his way in Stygian darkness, he was too relieved to be afraid.

The water grew deeper, the current of it stronger as he went a little uphill. As Ash had told him to, he bore always to the left.

His feet were numb beyond his ankles by the time he saw light ahead, but he had not had to travel as long as he had feared. With a shudder of relief he made his way onto a ledge and upward to an iron ladder. He grasped it and climbed to the passage above.

There were sounds ahead, footsteps. Henry

froze. Then he saw the pool of light on the dripping wall. Suddenly the slime of it was gold. A whole lantern appeared, and the hand holding it, then the sleeve of Squeaky's scorched and ruined jacket.

"Squeaky!" Henry shouted with joy. "Here! Over here!"

Squeaky came forward at a run, the lantern swinging around wildly, as his feet slid on the wet surface. "Where the hell have you been?" he demanded, his face contorted with both fury and relief. "You had us scared half to death! You ever do that again, an' I'll . . ."

Crow was coming behind him with Lucien and Bessie. They were all filthy, skin scratched and burned. Their clothes were torn and in some places blackened by fire, but they were alive.

Bessie threw her arms around Henry, hugging him with more strength than he would have thought she could possess. Slowly he closed his arms around her and held her just as powerfully.

"You need to get those burns tended," Crow interrupted. "We should get out and find clean water, bandages."

"Yes," Henry agreed. "Yes, of course." Now that he thought of it, parts of him hurt appallingly.

Even in the semi-darkness here, he felt as if he was still on fire. He let Bessie go at last and tried to collect his wits.

Crow took him by the arm, but holding only the cloth of his sleeve, not touching his skin. "Come on. Lucien knows the way."

It seemed like a long time, but perhaps it was no more than half an hour before they were standing in the street. The lamps were lit and gleaming in the dark, shedding pools of gold on the snow. Icicles sparkled from roofs and gutters. There were a few carriages and hansoms around, and they could hear harnesses jingling, hooves muffled in the snowdrifts that were still fresh and untrampeled.

In the distance people were singing.

Crow, the least disreputable-looking among them, hailed a cab. They all piled in, although with difficulty. Henry needed a little assistance.

"Where to?" Crow asked.

Henry gave him James Wentworth's address.

Lucien began to protest.

"According to the driver, it's Christmas Eve," Henry told him sharply. "You're going home. Where you go after that you can choose, but tonight you owe us this."

Lucien sat stiff and afraid, but he did not argue.

It was not a long ride to Kensington, where James Wentworth lived, but to Henry, who was exhausted and very sore, it seemed to take ages; Only now, on the brink of impossible success, did he actually wonder if Wentworth really wanted his son back to forgive him. Perhaps it would instead involve some harsher discipline, some price for his disobedience and the family's shame.

When they stopped they had to fish between them for enough coins to pay the fare and offer the cabbie a bonus fit for Christmas Eve. They climbed out stiffly, helping each other, until they stood on the freezing pavement. The hansom jingled and rattled off into the distance.

The street was lit as far as they could see in both directions. There were wreaths and garlands on the doors. Somewhere far away church bells were ringing out across the rooftops.

Henry walked up the short distance to Wentworth's door, lifted the brass knocker, and then let it fall.

The door was opened almost immediately and the liveried butler stared in undisguised disbelief.

Lucien stepped forward. "Happy Christmas, Dorwood. Is my father at home?"

The butler gasped and his eyes filled with tears. "Yes, Mr. Lucien," he said gravely. "If you care to come in, sir, I shall tell him you are here." He did not even bother to ask who his companions were.

Inside, the magnificent hall was decked for Christmas, as if they had been expected. The Yule log was burning in the open hearth. There were garlands of holly, ivy, and mistletoe, with colored ribbons. Red wax candles glowed. There was mulled wine in a large bowl on the sideboard, and cakes and pies and candied fruit in dishes.

A door flew open. James Wentworth came out, his eyes wide, his face shining with joy. He went straight to Lucien and threw his arms around him, too filled with emotion to speak.

Then he let him go and turned to Henry, the tears wet on his cheeks.

"Nothing I can say is thanks enough." He all but choked on the words. "My son was lost, and you have found him for me—you and your friends. My home and all that is in it are yours." He looked questioningly at each of them.

"My friends," Henry introduced them. "Dr. Crow, Mr. Robinson, and Bessie."

Bessie curtsied, with a slight wobble. Crow stood beaming the widest smile of his life, and Squeaky bowed, really rather gracefully.

"How do you do," Wentworth replied. "Happy, happy Christmas."

ABOUT THE AUTHOR

Anne Perry is the bestselling author of seven earlier holiday novels—*A Christmas Promise, A Christmas Grace, A Christmas Journey, A Christmas Visitor, A Christmas Guest, A Christmas Secret,* and *A Christmas Beginning*—as well as the William Monk series and the Charlotte and Thomas Pitt series set in Victorian England; the Byzantine historical epic *The Sheen on the Silk;* and five World War I novels. Anne Perry lives in Scotland.

www.anneperry.net

ABOUT THE TYPE

This book was set in Century Schoolbook, a member of the Century family of typefaces. It was designed in the 1890s by Theodore Low DeVinne of the American Type Founders Company, in collaboration with Linn Boyd Benton. One of the earliest types designed for a specific purpose, the *Century* magazine, it maintains the economy of a narrower typeface while using stronger serifs and thickened verticals.